V for Victory

Also by Teresa R. Funke

For adults and teens:

Dancing in Combat Boots
and Other Stories of American Women
in World War II

Remember Wake

For younger readers:

The Home-Front Heroes Books

Doing My Part

The No-No Boys

**Visit Teresa's interactive website at
www.teresafunke.com to:**

- Participate in fun Home-Front Heroes
  activities

- See pictures and read more about the real
  Home-Front Heroes

- Add your stories or your family's stories
  about the past

- Find out how to schedule Teresa to speak at
  your school or visit via webcast

To Sterling –

V for Victory

Be Victorious!
Teresa Funke

Teresa R. Funke

VICTORY
HOUSE
PRESS

Published by:

Victory House Press
3836 Tradition Drive
Fort Collins, Colorado 80526
www.victoryhousepress.com

Library of Congress Control Number 2009936386

Printed in the United States of America

ISBN 978-1-935571-12-4

To my father, who corrected my grammar
and taught me to love books

Acknowledgments

People often think authors write books all by themselves. They imagine me tucked away in some dusty corner, huddled over my computer keyboard or pad of paper. But writers need lots of people to help bring their books to print and keep them from getting lonely or discouraged while they work.

First, a writer needs her family. My family consists of my amazing husband, Roger, and my three talented children, Brian, Lydia, and Ava. They ask about my work every day and curl up on the bed with me at night to read the early drafts of my books and tell me what they think. And my parents, brother, aunts, and in-laws support everything I do. For this book, I most needed my great aunt, Lydia Treviño de Alonzo, who told me stories about running her brother's grocery store during World War II. It was uncommon in that time period for a woman to have such an important role in a neighborhood, but my aunt is very smart and kind and hard working, and she did her job well. So many of the details of how the grocery store in this book looked and how it was run came from my aunt. There would be no *V for Victory* without her or without my uncle, Roman, whom you'll learn more about in the back of the book.

And a writer needs other writers who can provide feedback and encouragement as the story develops. Writers like my fellow members of the Slow Sand Writers Society: Colleen Fullbright, Jean Hanson, Kathy Hayes, Luana Heikes, Sara Hoffman, Paul Miller, Kay Rios, and Debby Thompson. And, of course, my writing partner, Karla Oceanak, who has read and edited these pages so many times she practically has this story memorized.

A writer need friends. When you're not sure you're on the right path or that you'll ever be able to finish, you need people to say, "You can do it!" My friends Trai Cartwright, Marilee Morley, and Susan Skog boosted me up whenever I was frustrated.

Most writers need experts. When you write historical fiction, as I do, you have to guess at things you've never experienced. I do the best research I can using books, documents, personal accounts, live interviews, and the internet, but sometimes I *still* can't find the details I need. That's when I turn to the people who know that time period or subject or city better than I do. In this case, the people who helped the most were Tom Shelton at the Institute of Texan Cultures, Paula Allen, who writes a history column for the *San Antonio Express-News*, and Kenny Parnell, a fountain of information about San Antonio and its movie theaters as well as a fascinating man who would have made a great subject for one of my books. My friend and fellow author Laura Resau and her good friend Gloria Diaz helped me so much with the Spanish translations in this book.

A writer needs talented partners. People like Kendra Spanjer, my illustrator, who took my stick-figure suggestions for the cover and turned them into art, and Launie Parry, who wove Kendra's illustration into the cool design on the cover, and Erin Rogers, who worked to make sure the inside of the book was fun to look at and easy to read.

Lastly, a writer needs readers. My stories exist only in my head and on the page until you, dear reader, pick up my books. Then they come alive in your imaginations in ways I never dreamed of. We work magic, you and me. Thank you for the magic!

1

The Contest

The Empire Theatre is packed to the rafters with
kids. Up in the balconies, they rain candy wrappers
and spitwads down on us kids below. But when the
theater manager steps out on the stage and raises his
arms, we settle down. We know what's coming.

"Ladies and gentlemen, boys and girls," he says
into a microphone. "Have we got a treat for you!"

We're scooching to the edges of our seats now,
ready to jump up.

"Today we bring you, all the way from
Hollywood, California, everyone's favorite singing
cowboy, *Roooy Rogerrrs*!"

The huge movie screen starts to rise, and the
manager hurries offstage.

And there he is in the center of the stage, the
king of cowboy movies, Roy Rogers himself, sitting
atop his palomino horse, Trigger, who nods his head
to the crowd, his front hoof pawing the ground.

And the noise in the Empire is thunderous. Kids are clapping and stomping their feet. "Hey, Roy! Hey, Roy,!" they yell, hoping he'll look their way. I glance way up to the painted sky on the ceiling, half expecting it to crack down the middle.

My best friend, Gary, is hootin' and hollerin' as loud as anyone. He's waving his white cowboy hat, which is too small for him now. At twelve, almost thirteen, we're a little older than most of the kids in the theater today and probably too old to be wearing cowboy stuff, but I've got my fake sheriff's badge pinned to my shirt and a yellow bandanna tied around my neck, and Gary has his cowboy hat and a real Western-type shirt with fringe that his grandmother sewed for him. It's Roy Rogers, after all!

Roy tips his hat to the audience and does some riding tricks on Trigger while singing a song, then he jumps down and starts his rope tricks, which is what Gary and I came to see. "This one's called the Butterfly," he says as his rope spins small loops on either side of his body. "And this one's the Texas Skip." His loop grows larger, and he jumps right through the center of it. All of us kids watch in silence as he shows us a few more tricks then drops his rope to his side, doffs his hat, and gives us a sweeping bow. Then we all go wild again.

"Boy, that was something, wasn't it, Miguel?" Gary says, dropping into his seat like he's just run a race. He's got a dopey grin on his face. It's not every day you see your movie idol. At least not here in San Antonio. "That was *really* something." He's still shaking his blond head in disbelief.

I just nod. And that's all we say as we listen to the hum of excited voices bouncing off the gilded walls of the movie theater. One little kid in front of us is crying into his mother's arm. "I want him back," he's sobbing, and we think he means Roy, but then he says, "Bring the horsey back. Bring the horsey back," and we start to mimic him. His mother scowls at us over her shoulder, and we slouch back into our seats. A stagehand has finished sweeping the stage, though there was nothing to sweep up, from what I could tell. Can you imagine a horse like Trigger leaving a mess behind? Just never would happen.

As the theater manager struts onstage again, someone throws a balled-up candy wrapper at him, and he scoops it up in his fist, shaking it. "Okay now, kids, we've all had our fun. Now you need to settle down. I mean it! I won't tolerate any misbehavior."

He says this every week, but no one ever listens

11

to him.

"And no smoking in the balcony. You kids give us any trouble, my boys will kick you out."

He means his ushers, high school boys with flashlights who patrol the aisles snapping their fingers at kids to get them to shut up or to take their shoes off the backs of the seats. We pull our feet down till they go by, then put them up again, but we never mouth off to the ushers, 'cause they'll kick you out for that. They think they're big cheeses.

"Now, listen kids. I said *listen*," the theater manager shouts. "I'll have a special announcement after the second feature today, so boys and girls, make sure you stay in your seats. You won't want to miss this."

Gary and I grin at each other. Special announcements often mean something good. A contest or a giveaway or a live appearance, like today.

"Maybe it'll be a yo-yo contest again," Gary says. "You should enter this time, Miguel. You Walk the Dog better than anyone!"

"Nah, my brother, Ernesto, is the best. He's the one who taught me all those tricks, you know?"

"Well, he ain't here, and he's too old anyway. You should enter."

12

"They haven't even said what it's gonna be yet, Gary. Maybe the announcement's just some fluff about a war bond drive."

"Well, we'll find out after the show," he says as the lights dim. When the theater goes dark, we hear the crackling sound that comes at the start of a picture, then a blast of loud music as a flickering image with headlines fills the screen. It's the newsreel about to start. The little kids groan. They're impatient for the Donald Duck cartoon. But we older kids tell them to shush. Most days, we don't pay too much attention to what's happening in the war—not like the grown-ups do. We don't read the newspapers or listen to the reports on the radio, but we all watch the newsreels. I pay special attention to the footage of the planes and the battleships. Gary and I can name every plane the military is using. The slick fighter planes, the heavy bombers, the bulky cargo planes. We know them by sight when they fly over our city from the nearby bases. So it's always exciting to see them in battle on the newsreels. Maybe some of those pilots trained right here in Texas! And now, like Ernesto, they're over there fighting the Nazis and the Japanese.

After the newsreel comes the cartoon, then the serial. Now we're finishing up the first main feature—

an old Roy Rogers's picture in honor of his visit—but I've gotta go to the bathroom—bad. That's always a problem on these long afternoons, and the trick is to time it right so you don't miss the best parts of the show, but I didn't do that today.

"Doggone it," I say to Gary. "Tell me what happens."

I double-time it up the aisle and down to the basement bathrooms. When I'm finished, I'm tempted to run next door to the drugstore to buy some more popcorn, but they're almost to the part with the big stagecoach chase scene, and I don't want to miss that.

After the second feature finally wraps up, many of the kids get up to leave, but the theater manager comes back onstage waving his arms. He tells us to sit down, but we're not about to do that again. We've been sitting for hours.

"This is it," Gary says. "It better be good."

It doesn't sound good at first. The manager's announcing a scrap metal drive to help the war effort, and that's no big deal. The theater sponsors scrap metal or rubber matinees sometimes where you get in free if you bring two pounds of rubber or twenty-five pounds of scrap metal, like old pots and pans, which the government melts down to build planes and tanks and stuff. "Oh but wait," the manager is saying. "This isn't your ordinary scrap matinee. This is a contest, and it's going to last three weeks. At the end of the three weeks, the kid who brings in the most scrap metal is not just going to get a free pass to the movies, but a twenty dollar prize."

"Twenty dollars! Do you know what we could get for that kinda dough?" Gary says.

The movies are over, and we've left the theater and stopped at the soda fountain in Sommers Drugstore. We're sipping five-cent Coca-Colas, one of our favorite traditions after the matinees. "You can't beat a Coke," we like to say, just like the ad.

"Twenty bucks," Gary says again, letting out a long, low whistle.

I tip my glass and slurp the bottom clean with my straw. "If I had twenty dollars, I'd buy me a bicycle," I say. "Then I could get a paper route."

"My brother had a paper route," Gary says. "He quit it."

"Why?"

"Well, it sounded kinda fun at first, you know? You get a bike with those saddle bags over the back wheel all piled up with newspapers. Then you ride around tossing papers onto people's porches. But then you gotta go by their houses every week and try to catch them at home to pay the bill. And if they're not home, you gotta go back. And sometimes they are home, but they tell you to scram anyway. But what really got him was when it rained. And lots of the streets on his route weren't paved, you know, so he was pushing that heavy bike loaded down with papers through muddy streets. That was it for him."

I slurp some more, even though all the Coke in the glass is long gone now. I just like the sound. "Yeah, well, I'd still like a bike. Maybe I could use it to make deliveries for our store and my parents would pay me more. What would you do with twenty dollars?"

"Buy as many model airplanes as I could."

"But you already own just about every one ever made."

"Shows what you know. They've got new war planes coming out."

"We better go," I say. "It's getting late."

At the bus stop, we wait our turn as soldiers and sailors in uniform offer help to women carrying shopping bags and packages from the downtown stores. A couple of the older boys from our neighborhood line up behind us. When the bus driver motions us to hurry on, one of the boys pushes past and says, "Outta my way, Cueball." That's a nickname I've carried around the neighborhood for years because my mother keeps my hair so short I'm nearly as bald as a cueball in a game of pool. It saves us money, she says, because we don't need to pay the barber as often for a haircut. But I hate the nickname, and I hate the haircut too. It makes my ears stick out even farther.

The bus is so crowded we have to stand. Luckily the older boys move toward the center. I hear them laughing, and I hope it's not at me. They get off at a stop well short of our neighborhood, and I wonder what they're up to. But as soon as they leave, I find that I can concentrate again. And as we ride back to the East Side, I come up with a brilliant plan.

"Hey, Gary," I say. "What if we team up? We'll both get as much scrap metal as we can, but then only one of us will turn it in. Then we can share the twenty dollars. That way we're sure to win."

"But if we split the money, you can't get your bike."

I hadn't thought of that. "What if we bought the bike and we shared it? You'd get it for a week, then me."

Gary scratches his head, considering. I know he's thinking about those model airplanes.

"Ah, come on, Gary. It'll be fun. I'll even let you have the bike for the first week."

"Oh all right," he says. "I'll meet you tomorrow after church and we can start scouring the neighborhood. We'll start at the junkyard."

"Nah, that's too picked over, and every kid on the block is gonna head there. We need to think of places no one's thought of before."

"Like where?"

"I don't know. Come by the store and we'll figure it out."

Gary waves good-bye to me at the bus stop. As I'm passing the hardware store, a plane roars overhead. I glance up. "B-24," I say. It's not hard to spot the silhouette of that big bomber. When my gaze comes back down, I catch a glimpse of the stand-up clock inside the window of the store. It's almost seven o'clock! I've stayed much later than I was supposed to. I'm going to be in deep Dutch when I get home.

2

J. Montoya Grocery

"*Ay*, Miguelito," my aunt Silvia says when I come skidding in the front door of our grocery store. "Where have you been?"

"At the movies, Tía Silvia. It's Saturday."

"You were supposed to come home after the second feature today, remember? Your *mamá* wants your help closing the store."

"But we had to stay to hear the announcement, Tía. There's going to be a scrap metal drive at the Empire! And they're giving twenty dollars to the kid who brings in the most scrap. Gary and I are going to try to win it together and split the money! I was thinking —"

"You were thinking you could get the sawdust and spread it on the floor. Pronto."

"But don't you want to hear what I'm gonna do?"

"All I want to hear is the sawdust bucket scraping across the floor."

"Can't I at least eat dinner first? I haven't had anything but popcorn and Coke all day!"

Tía Silvia puts her hands on her hips and cocks her head at me. I get this look a lot. "Okay, but make it quick."

I dash out back and across the yard to the house we share: my parents; my grandparents; my older sister, Juanita; and now my brother's wife, Rosa, and her baby, Victor. There's a lot of us, but it's war time, so we make room for each other. And it's a big enough house. Two stories high! I even had my own room before Rosa and baby Victor moved in. Now he's bunking with me, and Rosa is sharing with Juanita. When this war is over, though, my brother, Ernesto, will come home and the three of them will get their own place again.

Ernesto's a co-pilot on a bomber flying over Nazi territory. Papá says he'd been crazy about planes ever since he was a little boy. He started taking flying lessons at Stinson Field when he was still in high school, before the war started. He paid for the lessons himself with the money he made at the store and from a second job as a waiter at the diner down the street. Even with two jobs, he still got better grades than I'm getting.

We're all pretty proud of Ernesto. We've hung a blue star in our kitchen window and another at the store so everyone knows we've got a man in the war, and I keep a picture of him on my nightstand. It shows him standing in his flight suit and bomber jacket with his crew beside their plane, Lady Victory. Victor likes to look at the picture. I think he thinks they named the plane after him. Maybe they did. I tell him it's his daddy in the picture, but I'm not sure he understands. He wasn't even born yet when Ernesto signed up after Pearl Harbor. Rosa missed my brother so much that she named the baby Victoriano, hoping for a quick victory in the war so Ernesto could come home. We call him Victor for short, and he's one and a half now and a mountain of trouble. Sometimes I think this little tank could take on the whole German army by himself. He latches onto my leg as soon as I come in the back door, and I have to drag him along with me as I move toward the stove.

"*¿Que hay de cenar, Abuelita?*" I ask, which is Spanish for "What's for dinner, Grandma?" Neither of my grandparents speak English. She's made some kind of vegetable stew, and it smells wonderful. I try to sneak a peek in the pot, but she hustles me out of the way as she fills my bowl and takes it to the table. I snag a *tortilla* off the stack in the warming oven and bend down to peel Victor off my leg. He reaches his pudgy arms up, opening and closing his fingers like he's asking for some of my food, his big, brown eyes pleading. "Not a chance, kid. You already ate. I can tell by the food smeared all over your face."

"Why don't you clean him up then?" my sister Juanita says, coming into the room. She's nineteen now and all gussied up for the evening. She's done her hair and is wearing her favorite dress and a new, V-shaped silver pin on her blouse. She must have half a dozen V for Victory pins by now, some store-bought, some homemade, and some given to her by soldiers or sailors she has danced with. She's clipping on earrings and swaying as if she can already hear the music.

"You clean him up," I say. "I'm eating."

"Nope. You're in charge of him tonight. Rosa, Silvia, and I are going to the dance at the USO."

"What? No! Why can't Mamá watch him?"

"She and Papá are going to the Alvarez's for a cocktail party. So that leaves you."

"But no one asked me! Maybe I've got plans of my own."

"You're twelve," she snorts. "What kind of plans could you have?"

"Quiet, both of you," Mamá says from the doorway. "Miguel, you *will* watch your nephew *after* you get your chores done at the store. Go now. And don't forget to lock the back door when you're done."

I'll argue with my sister, but not my mother. But I groan as I leave the table so they'll know I'm unhappy. I drift back across the yard, even though my mother told me to hurry. Overhead, a plane flies by on its way back to the base. It's growing dark, so I can't say for sure which kind it is, but the high-pitched buzz of the engine makes me think it's probably a P-51. One thing's for sure, it's not big enough to be a bomber like my brother flies.

If Ernesto were here, he'd side with me tonight about Victor. Though he was almost ten when I was born, he never bossed me around the way Juanita does. He was always my protector. But he's gone, off doing important things. And when they're not at the store, Juanita is off dancing with soldiers and helping with the Red Cross blood drives, and Rosa is volunteering at the hospital. After the war started, our delivery boys joined up, so Papá does all the deliveries now. That leaves Mamá to run the store, and now she hardly has time for me. Everyone has something important to do for this war except me. All I get to do is watch an ornery one-year-old. But they'll notice me more when I win that scrap metal contest.

And I'm *not* giving Victor a ride on my new bike.

We've been to church and back for an hour now and still no sign of Gary. He better not have forgotten. I'm leaning up against the counter with my arms folded, so I'll look good and annoyed when he finally comes in. My mother nudges me as she passes. The store is closed now, but Mamá and the girls are tidying up before the new week starts. "Here," Mamá says, handing me a pail of water, a rag, and a squeegee. "Wash the outside of the windows, please."

"But Mamá, I'm waiting for Gary. We're going to gather scrap. Remember, I told you about the contest?"

"When you're finished, you can leave."

"But he'll be here any minute!"

"Then it's a good thing you're such a fast worker," she says, pulling me toward her so she can kiss the top of my head. "And don't forget the front door."

Our store is called J. Montoya's Grocery, after my father, Jorge Montoya. It's painted yellow on the outside because Papá thought the color looked festive and would make people want to shop here. Papá had a lot of good ideas when he opened this store, and that's why he's one of the most popular neighborhood grocers in town. Just before the war started, we modernized the store. Our vegetables are fresh from the market each morning, and we bought a newfangled mister that keeps them fresh and cool. We have shopping carts with wheels and a brand new National cash register. We carry the most popular items and have the biggest and best selection of meat that rationing will allow. Everyone speaks well of our store and my family, and everyone is welcome here: Anglos, Mexicans, coloreds. We treat everyone with respect. My mother insists on it.

So while I'm washing the windows, people passing on the street are calling out to me, "*¡Buenas tardes,* Miguel!" I have to make a point to answer back because Mamá might be watching me through the window. But as I work, I steal glances down the street looking for Gary. I finally see him coming, wearing his Boy Scout uniform and pulling a Radio Flyer wagon. And he's got something else with him.

Alejandro. He's a kid from my school who lives near Gary and tags along with us whenever he can. He's wearing his Boy Scout uniform too. They're in the same troop. I dropped out last year because Mamá needed my help at the store after school, so I couldn't make the troop meetings anymore.

"What's with the uniforms?" I ask.

"As Boy Scouts and also Junior Commandos," Gary says, "it's our duty to collect scrap for the war effort."

"But your troop isn't turning in this scrap. *We* are," I say with a glance at Alejandro that lets him know we're not sharing with him.

"Yeah, but this way we look more official. Maybe people will give us more scrap."

"Yeah, people like Boy Scouts," Alejandro says.

I frown. It's not that I don't like Alejandro; it's just that he has a habit of coming between me and Gary, like he's doing right now.

"Fine," I say. "But we're following *my* plan today. Here," I shove the squeegee at Alejandro. "Help me finish up."

Mamá opens the front door and leans out. She's holding Victor, who is struggling to get down. Victor hates being carried. Mamá smiles at Gary and

Alejandro. "How are you, boys?"

"Fine, Mrs. Montoya," they answer in unison.

"Well good. Gary, tell your mother I said hello."

"Yes ma'am."

Mamá steps forward and drops Victor into my arms. "Take your nephew with you. We've got work to do."

"But Mamá, he's too heavy, and he'll get in the way."

"Nonsense. Put him in Gary's wagon. He'll enjoy that."

"But –"

"No buts, *mijo*. Bring him back by one o'clock, and I'll put him down for his nap."

"Arrgh." I drop Victor into the wagon, and he squeals with delight. He starts rocking back and forth, like he's trying to get the wagon moving, and he's got a big, slobbery grin on his face. Gary, Alejandro, and I just look at him with disappointment.

"Where do we start?" Gary asks with a sigh. "You wanna knock on doors?"

"Nah, I had an idea this morning." I lean in close like they do in the spy movies. "Let's try the convent."

"The nuns!" Alejandro says. "I'm not going

there."

"But that's the point. Most kids wouldn't go to the nuns, and we gotta think of places no one else has been."

"Okay, let's go," Gary says. Gary's got no reason to be afraid of the nuns. He goes to the public school. But Alejandro and I have been taught by the Sisters of the Holy Ghost since first grade, and we've been punished more than once. In fact, just before school let out for the summer, Sister Frances caught us speaking Spanish at recess and made us kneel on the hardwood floor with our noses up against the blackboard for an hour. Spanish is not allowed at school. My knees ached for days.

I glance at Alejandro and realize he's remembering that wood floor too. "Come on, man," I say. "There's a war on. We gotta be brave."

Alejandro gives me a faint smile and falls in behind me.

When Gary yanks on the wagon handle, Victor topples back, but he doesn't cry. That's one good thing about the kid. He never cries.

"What kind of stuff you think the nuns got in there?" Alejandro asks.

"I don't know. Same as anybody. Pots, pans, metal

spoons, maybe some rusty garden tools. Nuns like to garden, you know."

"Maybe they've got some stuff other people don't have," Alejandro says. "Some nun things, you know?"

"Like what?"

"I don't know. Maybe some iron crosses or some broken rosary chains?"

"But you can't just melt down something holy like that," I say, "and then turn it into a bomb! That's gotta be against Church teaching, don't you think?"

"I don't know. Like you said, there's a war on," Gary says. "The country needs it, right? I mean, shouldn't we remind them the country needs it?"

Alejandro and I don't answer. We walk the rest of the way up the hill to the convent in silence, hoping the nuns *don't* give us anything that could get us in trouble with the Man Upstairs, as Father Donohue calls him. The only one of us who doesn't seem worried is Victor, who keeps getting up on his knees no matter how many times I set him back down. Well, it won't be my fault if he falls out. I didn't want to bring him anyway. And I've got bigger worries as we approach the convent.

3

The Crash

As we pass through the gate in the stone wall surrounding the convent, we see we aren't the only ones visiting the Sisters today. A guy about Juanita's age is coming down the stairs. He looks a little familiar, but I can't be sure. He's wearing an army uniform, and it takes me a minute to realize that his right shirt sleeve is pinned up to his shoulder. He must have lost his arm in the war. I find myself staring at his empty sleeve as we approach.

When I glance up into his face, he's glaring at me, and I feel my cheeks go red. He's caught me looking at him. He continues to glower at me as he passes us by.

"Who's that?" Gary asks.

"I don't know. But he looks familiar. I think he used to come into the store."

"I wonder what happened to his arm," Alejandro says.

"Why don't you go ask him," I snap, angry because it wasn't just me who noticed the soldier's arm, but it was only *me* the soldier glared at.

Alejandro and I leave Gary and Victor with the wagon and climb the stairs of the big, brick building. When we ring the bell, Sister Frances herself opens the huge door. We try not to fidget—nuns hate that— but it's hard, especially when she looks down her nose at us.

"Miguel, Alejandro, what brings you here this afternoon?" Her voice sounds a little lighter than it does in school.

"We're collecting scrap for the war effort, Sister," I say. "Would you have anything you could spare?"

"You boys come in, and I'll see what I can find for you."

Alejandro starts to step through the door, but I reach an arm out to stop him. "That's okay, Sister. We'll wait here." The last thing we need is to sit in a convent with a bunch of nuns. Sister Frances looks amused. "Suit yourself," she says. "I'll be right back."

When I turn around, Victor has crawled out of the wagon. He's pulling up flowers, and Gary is too busy watching us to notice. "Victor, no!" I cry, flying down the stairs to yank him away. So much for getting into Sister Frances's good graces. I try to pick Victor up, but he bats my hands away, and he's pretty strong for a little guy. So we form a triangle around him to keep him from wandering. He screams and tries to dodge between us, but we make a game of keeping him in. We're not trying to be mean, but it's funny watching him get mad, and we're so caught up in the game that we don't notice that Sister Frances has returned. She's come down the stairs and is depositing some scrap in the wagon. There's a pot and a broken ax head and a couple of bent spoons. And something that looks like a spittoon. But what would a spittoon be doing in a convent? I pick it up and consider it.

Sister Frances crosses her arms and looks down at me. "Sister Agatha used to spit tobacco juice. Nasty habit. I've been meaning to get rid of it since she passed away." She raises an eyebrow like she's daring me to say something. I set the spittoon down and pick up a roundish pan with a hole in the top. "Bedpan," she says. I've seen those in movies. They're for going to the bathroom in bed when you're too sick to get up. I drop it and wipe my fingers on my shirt. "We take care of our sick here, of course," Sister Frances says. "But I suppose we can spare one for the war effort." She arches that eyebrow again.

"Thanks, Sister," I say, busying myself with settling Victor amongst the junk in the wagon so I don't have to look her in the eyes.

"If you win that twenty dollars, I hope you'll keep the Church in mind," she says, turning back toward the gate.

"How'd she know we were trying to win the contest?" Gary whispers to me.

"How do nuns know anything? They just do."

A huge plane flies low over the convent. Victor reaches up for it. "Gooney Bird," Gary and I say, which is the nickname for the C-47, then we all hightail it down the hill, wanting to put some distance between us and the convent. Victor laughs as he and the first pieces of our scrap heap jostle around in the wagon.

We hit a few of the houses in the neighborhood, and people who've already dug deep for scrap look again. They come out with only little stuff: a broken alarm clock, a rusty pipe, a large ball of tin foil. We're not accomplishing much, and Victor is getting cranky. It's almost time for his nap, so we decide to take him back. As we're rounding the corner to our store, we're scheming how we can get old Mr. Garza to let us take apart the car he never drives anymore. Think of all the scrap that could bring in!

But then we hear a tremendous crash, and the windows on the houses rattle. We stop where we are. Everyone on the street has stopped too. There's a feeling that's spreading. Something bad has happened. Victor can sense it too. He starts to whimper. I go back to pick him up, and this time he doesn't protest. Then we see it: thick, black smoke billowing toward the sky. Someone screams, and then everyone starts running toward the smoke. We see my mother and sister come out of the store. Juanita doesn't even notice us as she rushes off in the direction everyone else is heading.

But Mamá stops a man rushing back the other way. "What is it?" she asks.

"Plane crash," the man says. "A couple of blocks away. Looks like the pilot lost control and crashed into a house. I'm going to call an ambulance."

Gary and Alejandro exchange a look and take off down the street. I try to hand Victor to Mamá so I can follow, but she pushes him back at me. "No, *mijo*, you stay here. Keep an eye on Victor and the store."

"But Mamá!"

"Do as I say," Mamá says.

"Ah, nuts!" I stomp into the store and dump Victor on the counter by the cash register and go back outside. I stand on my tiptoes as if I could actually see something. I barely notice the man who slips by me into the store.

I hear a thud and the sound of something rattling across the floor, and Victor says, "Uh, oh." He's knocked a five-pound bag of pinto beans off the counter. Mamá must have been filling the bag when she heard the crash. There are beans everywhere.

"Oh Victor," I cry. "Look what you did." I drop down to my knees to scoop up the beans.

"Look what *you* did," a voice says. "Left a baby on top of a counter. Not too swift, brother."

I glance up and see the soldier from the convent, the one with the missing arm. He's pushing beans toward me with his boot, and I don't appreciate the smirk on his face.

"Well, I shouldn't be here," I say. "I always get stuck with him. I wanna see what's going on."

"What's to see? A plane crashed. Very likely a man or two died. Lots of men die in this war."

I think of Ernesto when he says that, and my

stomach flips. I sit back on my heels and gaze up at the one-armed man. "You know, we're not open. It's Sunday. We close at noon on Sunday."

"That's okay. I'm just looking."

"Do I know you?" I ask.

"Not really. I knew your sister, though. Juanita. We were in high school together in our senior year."

"What's your name?"

"Alfonso. Alfonso Rivera."

I point at the chevron on his uniform sleeve. "Private Rivera."

His face clouds over. "Not anymore . . . You should quit feeling sorry for yourself and take that kid off the counter before he falls."

"You should mind your own beeswax," I say.

He glowers at me and turns away.

Just then, Gary skids to a stop outside the front door and waves me over. "Look what I got," he says. It's a piece of metal about the size of his fist. "It's from the plane."

He hands it to me, and I turn it over in my hand. It's warm to the touch. "You gonna put it on the scrap heap?"

"No siree, I'm keepin' this one. You should have seen it, Miguel. There were parts of the plane everywhere!"

"What kind of plane was it?"

"AT-18, I think. One of those advanced trainer planes."

Even I don't know much about those planes, but Gary does. Gary knows about every plane. "They're supposed to be hard to land," he says. "And lightweight and flimsy. Folks say the plane stalled and hit some power lines, then it slammed right into the roof of a house! The lady in the house got out, though. She was standing right beside me, watching her house burn." Gary shakes his head, and he doesn't look as excited anymore.

The soldier is over by the vegetable bins. I can feel him staring at me, and I know what he's waiting for me to ask.

"What about the crew?" I say.

"Don't know. . . Dead, I guess. Your mother wouldn't let me get close enough to see, and the smoke was too thick anyway."

The soldier comes up to the counter. His eyes are boring into me. He places a tube of Colgate Dental Cream on the counter.

"I can't help you," I say. "I'm not allowed to run the register yet."

"Then I'll wait," he says, but I wish he wouldn't. I don't like the way he's looking at me, like he can see right through me.

"Where's Alejandro?"

"His mother saw him at the crash site. Said he should go home."

"You should go too then," I say to Gary, handing him back the piece of plane. "Don't forget the wagon."

"Don't you wanna go around some more?"

"Nah, I don't feel like it. 'Sides, I got work to do."

Gary shrugs his shoulders. "See you tomorrow then."

As he's leaving, I hear Juanita's voice and snatch Victor off the counter as Mamá and Juanita come in. I don't ask them what they saw. They drift right past me and don't even notice the soldier. Mamá goes to the stepstool we keep behind the counter and sits down, her head in her hands. Juanita stands beside her, her eyes fixed on the floor.

I cross my arms and glare at the soldier as if to say *I told you so. No one's going to help you.*

"I'll be back later," he says, leaving the dental cream on the counter. I hope he doesn't come back. That guy gives me the willies.

4

Un Nombre Fuerte

An article ran in the *San Antonio Express* this morning about yesterday's crash. Turns out the co-pilot was from San Antonio. In fact, his family lives not too far from us. Mamá says she remembers him from when he was a kid. Gary called to tell me he thinks they were flying low so the co-pilot could show the pilot our neighborhood. Gary says that's why they never station pilots near their hometowns, so nothing like this will happen. But the pilots were supposed to be delivering the plane to Laredo, and no one knows why they asked to land here instead. Mamá cut out the article and set it on the kitchen table. Every time she passes it, she gets tears in her eyes. Maybe she's thinking about Ernesto, hoping the same thing won't happen to him.

I've been moping around too since the crash. I've barely said a word to anyone, but no one seems to have noticed. They're all caught up in their own thoughts. Well, maybe one person has noticed: Abuelo, my grandfather. He comes into my room after I go to bed and taps my foot. "Come with me to *el mercado* tomorrow," he says in Spanish.

I groan. Abuelo goes to the market at six o'clock every morning to pick out the freshest fruits and vegetables for our store. I don't want to be *anywhere* at six in the morning. "Come on, Miguelito. We'll have some fun."

What does he mean by "fun," I wonder as I get dressed the next morning. I'm still yawning as I stumble down the stairs into the kitchen. Mamá sends me to fetch the keys to the truck from Papá. I find him working on the account books in the back room of the store as he does every morning, but when I open my mouth to speak, a giant yawn comes out instead. Papá laughs.

"Look at you, up so early," he teases. "Off to *el mercado*? Tell Abuelo to skip the beets today. Just because they're his favorite doesn't mean they sell well." He winks and tosses me the keys. I barely catch them, I'm still so tired.

Abuelo and Mamá are waiting for me in the delivery truck. The words J. Montoya Grocery are painted on the doors. My father believes in advertising. We drive to the market in silence. Mamá stares straight ahead. It's like she's a thousand miles away lately, and it kinda worries me, but as we near the market, she pins her hat on and smoothes the folds of her dress, and her soft smile reassures me. We climb out of the truck into the vibrant mood of the market, and Abuelo puts on his jacket. Abuelo always wears a suit and tie, even in the heat of summer. He's a proud man.

The farmers's stalls are set up around the square. Abuelo is very selective, and he takes his time. He likes the looks of the potatoes today, and the onions. He always buys tomatoes. They sell well in the store. He doesn't approve of the carrots, though, and we still have some left from yesterday, and luckily, he passes on the beets. The only fruit he'll consider is a box of apricots from one of the vendors. He waves away another farmer who tries to sell him bruised peaches and another who offers him overripe melons at a discount. Nothing but the best in our store. When we're finished, Abuelo and I load the boxes and sacks onto the bed of our truck. Mamá has made a few purchases of her own, some molasses candy she'll sell in the store and a couple of *piñatas* she'll hang in the front window.

Mamá goes around to the passenger side, but Abuelo hands her the keys to the truck instead. "Miguel and I have some errands to run," he says.

Mamá looks perplexed then smiles faintly and pulls me over for that kiss on the head. I've told her I'm getting too old for that, but she doesn't listen. "Behave yourself," she says.

"Where are we going, Abuelo?" I ask.

"Mi Tierra." This is our favorite restaurant. They open early for the farmers, and it's a special treat to eat there. My grandfather has only taken me twice before. My favorite dish is *cabrito*, baby goat, but it's probably too early in the day for that. Abuelo suggests we share the steak and eggs, so I agree, my mouth watering at the delicious smells coming from the kitchen.

As we finish our food, my grandfather sips his *café con leche* and eyes me. "Did you know I chose your name?" he asks me in Spanish.

I shake my head, surprised.

"*Sí*. Miguel: the archangel, powerful, strong. When I held you for the first time, this is how you felt to me. Strong. A strong grip, strong legs. I told your father, this boy needs *un nombre fuerte*, a strong name."

"Well, the only thing I seem to be strong enough to do these days is lug around Victor. Why can't I do more at the store? I'm old enough. I'd rather do that than watch a runny-nosed kid."

"What would you do at the store if you could?"

"Run the cash register. Then Tía Silvia or Juanita could watch the baby."

"Making change takes concentration, and your mind is always off with your friends. You don't have the knowledge yet to run the cash register."

"Then why can't I help more with deliveries?"

"You're not old enough to drive. And we don't need two people in a truck to make deliveries."

"Well, it doesn't take much strength to run a feather duster or put price stickers on cans. When will I be old enough to do something more important?"

He doesn't answer me directly. Instead, he says, "When your *papá* was your age, he used to help me in our *tienda* in Mexico, our dry goods store. Those were hard times, and then we lost everything in *la Revolución*. We came to America so our grandchildren would have a better life, wouldn't have to work so hard or get by with so little. Helping your family is important. *Es lo primero*. Mind your *mamá*, mind your aunt. That's all, Miguel. That's enough."

He's gazing at me over the top of his coffee cup, and now I know why he brought me here. Just like my mother, he's trying to tell me to behave, to quit complaining. I can't catch a break from anyone. No one ever told Ernesto he wasn't old enough or good enough to do those things. Just me.

Abuelo must read the disappointment on my face because he stands and pulls me up gently by my shirt. "Come on, boy. I'm in the mood for *pan dulce*. Let's pick out some pastries to take home to the women."

We walk to the nearby *panadería*, the bakery. With the sugar shortage, they don't offer the variety they once did, but they still make my favorites, *empanadas de calabaza*, pumpkin turnovers, and Abuelo's favorite, *empanadas de camote*, sweet potato turnovers. After we leave the *panadería*, Abuelo suggests we visit the spice shop. Abuelita is running low on *comino* and oregano, and this spice shop is the best in town. On the way to the bus, I think of something I want to buy. Some tissue paper for a kite I'm making, one last fun thing to do before school starts in three weeks. I have a kite, but I've patched it so many times it won't fly anymore. I tell Abuelo, and he steers me toward the drugstore. I pick out the paper, and then Abuelo surprises me with some balsa wood for the frame. I'd been using twigs before. "This will work better," he says. "*Yo te lo compro.*"

"Thank you!"

He rubs my stubbly head, and after we've paid, hands me all the packages to carry. As we're walking toward the bus stop, a troop train pulls through town. Men in uniform are leaning out the windows, calling to the passersby, whistling at the ladies, and waving to anyone who will wave back. I trot alongside the train a few paces. It's moving slowly because it's in town, but I can't wave back because of the packages. "Hey, kid," one of the soldiers yells. "Got anything good in that sack?"

"*Empanadas.*"

"Won't be any of those where we're going. Take it easy, kid."

Abuelo catches up to me. He doesn't raise his hand to wave. His face looks drawn as we watch the train roll by. "Many soldiers have I seen in my lifetime. You see, Miguelito, there is plenty of time to be a man. For now, it's enough to be a boy." We catch the bus back to the store, and I show Mamá the fixings for my kite, but she's more excited about the sack of pastries and the spices, which she sets behind the counter. She looks happy for the first time since the plane crash.

Juanita takes down the feather duster from its peg and hands it to me. "Here, Miguel. Dust the cans."

I glance at Abuelo. He covers his mouth with his hand to hide his grin. I sigh and lean my bag of kite fixings in the corner. I take the duster from Juanita. Then something catches Abuelo's keen eye, and I follow his gaze. There's a girl a little older than me in the corner. She comes from a big family, and they've been known to steal. Abuelo throws me a knowing look and indicates with his finger that he's noticed her. As she passes him, he steps forward suddenly, bumping right into her. I hear a faint cracking sound, and the girl says, "Oh!" She steps back and looks at the front pocket of her skirt, which is now dripping something thick and yellow. Egg yolk! "*Ay, perdón, señorita*," my grandfather says. And the girl's face turns red. She bolts from the store. Abuelo chuckles quietly and throws me a wink. I'm about to laugh myself until I notice that someone else is watching too—the soldier with the missing arm.

"You shouldn't let her get away with stealing," he

says to me. "She'll only do it again."

"She didn't get away with it," I say. "We take care of things our own way here. You sure do like to stick your nose in where it doesn't belong."

"What else have I got to do?" he says, looking down at his missing arm.

"Ah, who's feeling sorry for himself now?" I say, breaking Mamá's rule of always talking nicely to the customers. But this guy's different. He gets under my skin somehow.

Alfonso's eyes narrow. He turns and storms out of the store.

"Miguel," my sister says. "What did you say to him?"

"Nothing. He's an odd duck, that's all."

Juanita doesn't look convinced, but then a woman taps her on the arm and asks for help finding foot powder. Juanita shakes a finger at me. I shrug to let her know I don't care. And I *don't* care . . . unless she tells Mamá. Then I'll care plenty.

5

A Way to Win

"Miguel, come here," Rosa says. She's balancing Victor on her hip, and I hold out my arms, assuming she wants to hand her son to me. But she shakes her head. "We're sending some letters to Ernesto, and your mother and I want you to write to him this time."

"Now?"

"Yes, of course now. Why?"

"The guys are coming over. We're going to the park to try out my new kite."

Victor has wrapped his hands in Rosa's hair, and she's struggling to untangle them. "Just write to your brother, Miguel. It won't take long."

"But Juanita's the letter writer. She must be writing to six soldiers by now," I say. "She says it's part of her war work. Keeping their spirits up and all that. Can't I tell Ernesto 'hi' in one of her letters? That's what I usually do."

"No, we want you to write your own."

"But I never know what to say!"

"You'll think of something." She sets Victor down and pulls a piece of V-mail stationery and a pencil from the drawer. "Here. If you hurry, you can finish before your friends come. I want to mail the letters today." She picks up Victor and heads to the back of the store. I tap the pencil against my temple, thinking, but nothing comes to me. Juanita will tell him all the good stuff, and Mamá will tell him about the store. Rosa will talk about Victor. School's not in, so I can't even tell him stories about the nuns. I could tell him about the plane crash, but I suppose I shouldn't. It might worry him. So there's nothing left for me to say, and the censors make me nervous anyway. Sister Frances explained to us in school that if we write anything "sensitive" in our letters, the military censors will cut it out. But I don't know what counts as sensitive. It's like that saying, "Loose Lips Sink Ships." Juanita says that means there could be spies anywhere, and if we say something important about the war, they could relay that information back to the Germans or the Japs. But what counts as important?

I glance up at the door, hoping Alejandro and

Gary have shown up to rescue me, but they're late as usual, so I put pencil to paper finally, and this is what I write:

Dear Ernesto,   *August, 1943*

I hope you are feeling well and doing lots of flying. Everyone here is sure worried about you. But I'm not. I know how tough you are. Remember when you stepped on that rusty nail? I was a little kid, but I remember. You didn't even cry. So I guess you can handle just about anything.

I'm waiting for Gary and Alejandro. We're going to go fly my new kite. I made it with balsa wood that Abuelo bought for me. We strung some rags together for the tail, but we'll see if it gets off the ground. There's a scrap metal contest, and Gary and I are trying to win. Can I say that in this letter? About the metal contest, I mean? Because we're doing it to help win the war so you can come home. Can I say that? About us winning the war? I'm not sure what to write in this letter. If we win the contest, we get twenty dollars. I was going to buy a bike with the money, but Abuelo says I'm getting old enough now to help the family more. So maybe I should give a couple of bucks to Rosa so she can buy some new clothes for Victor. That kid grows like a weed, and none of the women have time to sew anymore, except Abuelita, but her eyesight is bad. You shouldn't worry about Victor, though. I'll keep a good eye on him. Well, that's all I can think of.

Your brother, Miguel.

I read back what I wrote and think about erasing the part about the scrap metal drive. If my letter fell into the wrong hands, the enemy might know we're trying to help the war effort in San Antonio. But just then Gary and Alejandro burst in. They're laughing and pushing each other out of the way as they make a mad dash for the counter.

Gary slams his hand down first. "I win," he says.

"You cheated! You pushed me."

"You pushed me first. Admit it. I won."

"Fine, winner buys the candy."

Gary frowns. "I got no money. You buy the candy."

"I got none either."

They turn toward me. "Don't look at me. I'm not paying for nothing."

"Oh for heaven's sake," Rosa says with a smile.

"Here, take this and get out, all of you. You're scaring away the customers with your noise."

Gary holds out his hand but frowns at the molasses candy she lays in his palm. "Mrs. Montoya, when you gonna get good candy again? What I wouldn't give for a Hershey's bar."

"When the war is over, you can have all the chocolate you want. Until then, it goes to the soldiers. Everything we do is for them." Rosa's eyes mist, and Gary seems to remember my brother, off fighting. He mutters his thanks to Rosa then jerks his head toward the door, and I follow. I leave the letter on the counter.

We run around back to my house and pick up my kite. Abuelita asks where we are going, and I tell her we'll back soon. We leave before she can suggest we take Victor with us.

We race around the front of the store, nearly knocking into a group of older boys. Two of them are the boys who were on the bus. One of them reaches out and shoves me.

"Watch it, Cueball," he says. He's Tug, one of the Wagner boys.

"Sorry," I mumble as I try to step around him.

"What's the hurry?" Tug says, pushing me back

again.

"Yeah, and where's the red wagon?" one of the other boys asks. They must have seen us scouting for scrap the other day.

"Leave me alone," I say, but they're blocking me. Alejandro and Gary got past them from the start. They're waiting a little ways down the street for me, looking worried.

"What's the matter?" Tug says. "Scared?"

"Nah, I've just got things to do." I step to the left this time, but he steps with me.

"You ain't gonna win, you know."

"Win what?"

"The scrap contest. I've got it all sewn up. My uncle's furnace broke down. He's getting a new one, and I get to haul the old one in for scrap. You ever seen a furnace, Cueball? It's huge."

I look away so he won't see my reaction. I've always been a sore loser, and I'd especially hate to lose to a wise guy like this. But I'm not about to let him know it.

"Who cares about the crummy scrap drive," I say, looking him straight in the eye. "That's kid stuff. 'Sides, I think I see your father." He turns his head, and when he does, I duck around him quick as a fox.

I catch up to Gary and Alejandro and we run like the dickens, looking over our shoulders. But Tug and his friends haven't followed. We make it to the park and double over, out of breath.

"Well, there goes your bike," Alejandro says.

"Ah, twenty dollars would've only been enough for a kid's bike anyway," Gary says.

"I don't even know if I want a bike anymore. But I'm sure as shootin' not giving up now."

"But he's got a furnace," Gary says. "We can't beat that."

"Sure we can."

"How?" Gary crosses his arms, waiting for me to answer, and that makes me sore.

"I don't know. Why do I have to think of everything?"

Alejandro shrugs, and we all stand around for a minute staring at our shoes.

"Come on," Gary says finally. "Let's fly this dumb thing."

He reaches for the kite, and I hand it to him. Gary runs with the kite, and Alejandro trots along beside him. I hold the string. When he's far enough out, Gary tosses the kite in the air, where it sits for a minute on the breeze, looking beautiful. Alejandro pumps his arms up and down like he's pushing the kite higher. I pull on the string, trying to get it to rise, which it does, but then it turns and nosedives right into the ground. We all race to it, but the guys let me pick it up. It's my kite, after all. I'm lucky. There's only a slight tear in the tissue paper. I can patch that later. But the wood has held.

"The tail's too long," Alejandro says.

"No, there's not enough wind," Gary says.

"Maybe the rags are too heavy. We should cut one off," I suggest.

But Gary and Alejandro want to try again. They think maybe I didn't give enough tug to the string. I don't want to. Every time the kite crashes, we run the risk of the balsa wood splitting, but they insist on trying again. I give up talking them out of it, but I'm not gonna watch as they wreck my kite, so I cram my hands in my pockets and turn my back on them. I'm still fuming about Tug Wagner. Now it's not just about the twenty dollars. It's about beating him too, 'cause a kid like that isn't gonna do anything good with the money. He'll probably buy a BB gun and terrorize us all. I gotta figure out a way to beat a furnace, but how?!

I catch sight of a man cutting across the edge

of the park. It's Alfonso. He's carrying a paper sack, and he's all hunched over, like he doesn't feel good or something. I shade my eyes with my hands to cut the glare of the sun so I can see where he's going. He turns down a side street near the park.

"I'll be right back," I shout, and I follow Alfonso.

At the end of the street, I see him stop outside a small house with waist-high hedges on either side of the yard and a rusting piece of wrought-iron fence across the front. He struggles to hold onto the sack and open the latch on the gate with his one hand. I hadn't thought about how hard it must be to get by with only one arm until that moment. When he's through, the gate swings shut behind him with a loud creak. He starts up the walkway but doesn't go into the house. He gets in an old Ford coupe parked under a carport, but he doesn't start the car. He just sits there.

Gary and Alejandro come up behind me. "What're you doing?'

"I know that man," I say, pointing at Alfonso's car.

"So."

"So, take a look at his house! See anything useful there?"

"What?"

"The fence, dummy. A wrought-iron fence. Think how much scrap *that* could bring in! We get that fence, we might win."

"Well, you can't just ask him!"

"Why not? It's not even in good shape."

Gary looks at Alejandro for support, but Alejandro only shrugs. Then Gary squints toward the car again. "I don't know, Miguel. What's he doing? Why's he just sitting there? Something feels strange."

Gary's right, but I don't want to admit it. I don't want him to think I'm scared or nothing.

"I'm going to ask him."

"Go ahead," Gary says. "I'm staying here."

"Me too," Alejandro agrees.

"Fine. I'll do it myself."

I'm amazed how sure my voice sounds, because my feet don't feel sure at all. I have to coax them down the street. I open the gate and approach the car. I hesitate as I get closer, though. He's sitting so still, I can't tell what he's doing. I glance back at the street. Just as I thought, the guys have followed me, but they've stopped at the gate. Gary shakes his head, but that makes me want to do it just to show him. I've had enough of being pushed around for one day.

I step up and tap on the passenger door. The

windows are down, so Alfonso should have heard me coming, but he's staring straight ahead. I tap again, "Alfonso? It's Miguel. Juanita's brother." Still no movement. "From the store. J. Montoya's."

"I know which store," he says in a low growl. "What do you want?"

Now that it's time to say it, I realize what a crazy idea it is to think Alfonso will give me his fence.

"Whatcha doin'?" I say instead.

"I'm thinking about going for a drive," he answers with a sharp laugh. "But that's all I can do . . . *think* about it. Can't really drive with one arm, now can I? What do you want, kid?"

I glance back at Gary and Alejandro. I have the wild idea that if I can cheer Alfonso up, maybe then I can ask him for his fence. "How 'bout I help you?" I say. "You steer, and I'll shift. You can steer with one arm, right? My father does it all the time."

Alfonso turns to me. His eyes are red, and there are dark circles under them, like he hasn't slept in days. He needs a shave and probably a bath too. And there's the smell of something rotting coming from the bag. He squints at me, then lets out a long sigh. "Get in."

I hurry back to the gate and tell my friends where

I'm going. "Wait for me at the park," I say. "See if you can get the kite up without busting it to pieces. Here, take my pocketknife in case you need to shorten the tail."

"I don't like this," Gary says.

"It'll be fine. He used to know my sister." But not even Juanita talks to Alfonso now. He's just not the kind of guy you want to get to know.

Alfonso has started the engine. He's sitting up straighter now, and he gives me a long look as I climb in.

"You know what you're doing?" he asks.

"Sure. My brother Ernesto used to let me shift when I was younger."

"Where's he now?"

"He's stationed in England. He's a flyer."

"So, fine. Shift then."

I put the car in reverse, and we back out of the driveway.

"Where're we headed?" I ask.

"Nowhere."

I shift into first gear, then second as we start to meander through the streets of the neighborhood. Pretty soon we're heading toward the edge of town. This is farther than I thought we'd go, and I'm a little nervous. If Gary and Alejandro give up and go home, they'll tell my mother, and she won't like this one bit.

I try to think of something to say that will fill the eerie silence. "So, why'd you join up?"

"Why do you think?"

"To serve your country, I guess. That's why my brother did it."

"My country," Alfonso says with a sneer. "I was born in Mexico, but I don't remember it. I was only four when we came to America. But I was never treated like an American till the war started. They made me a citizen when I joined up. If a man's willing to die for a country, I guess they figure that proves his loyalty. Well, I was ready to die if I had to, but I wasn't ready for this." He glances down at his pinned-up sleeve. "We're going back." He jerks the wheel sharply to the left and steps on the gas. We're going faster than we should in town, and I hope no cops see us. Alfonso makes a hard turn into the driveway next to his house. He shuts off the car then grabs my arm suddenly, his face close to mine. "What did you come here for, Miguel? Tell me the truth."

"Well, there's this scrap drive, see. I thought . . . I thought maybe you could give up your fence."

He loosens his grip and tips his head back to let

out that sharp, hard laugh again. "I can't give you my fence, brother."

"Why not?"

"Just can't. Now go away, Miguel. Stay off my property." He shoves me out of the car. "I mean it."

"Fine," I say, slamming the door, embarrassed and annoyed. I just want to get away from him, but I turn at the corner to look back. He's gotten out of the car and is dumping the contents of his smelly bag into the next yard, where an eager cocker spaniel laps it up. Funny, I never would have thought of him as the type to care about a dog. I watch as he slumps up the porch steps into his house.

Gary and Alejandro are sitting under an elm tree, pulling up blades of grass. When they see me coming, they jump to their feet.

"What happened? Why were you gone so long?"

"Nothing happened. Let's go."

"Did you get the fence?" Gary asks.

"Forget about the fence," I say, gathering up the kite, which now has a pretty good tear in it. "I've got a better idea."

6

Mr. Garza's Jalopy

The next day, I ring up Gary, but he can't come by today. His mother is taking him to visit his grandmother.

"But you gotta tell me first," he says. "What's your big plan?"

"You'll see when you get back. But it's better than a furnace. Better than a fence even."

"Tell me."

"No," I laugh. "Come by when you get back. I'll show you."

Gary groans and hangs up on me. I finish my breakfast, eager to get started on my plan, but Rosa stops me in the doorway. "Miguel, I need you to watch Victor for a while. I have to go out."

"Can I watch him when I get back? I got something important to do!"

"Important?" she says, and I recognize that tone. She doesn't believe me. They never do. "Well, you can take him along with you then. Take the buggy if you want."

Oh that's just what I need, for Tug Wagner to see me pushing a baby carriage around. "No thanks, I'll carry him," I say, stomping over to where Victor is whacking two spoons together. I yank the spoons from his hand, and he does that loud squawk that nearly breaks your eardrums. I snatch him up, and he does his best to wriggle loose. But when he sees we're going outside, he settles down. "Out," he says in his baby voice. He's talking more now.

"Yeah, out," I say, boosting him up as I head down the alley toward Mr. Garza's house.

Mr. Garza is an old man, so old that most of his teeth are gone. He's lived by himself since his wife died. He's always outside, sitting in a frayed wicker chair beneath an oak tree, watching his yard. The street that runs in front of his house is pretty quiet, and there's a vacant lot opposite, so that's where we boys set up our baseball games some evenings. Mr. Garza always scoots his chair closer to the curb, just daring any of us to chase a ball into *his* yard. You could say Mr. Garza doesn't like kids much. But he's about my only hope.

"*Buenos días, señor,*" I say to him. I know Mr.

Garza can speak English well, but he might prefer Spanish, and I'm trying to get on his good side.

He leans forward in the chair and squints at me. "Stop right there," he says, and I wait on the sidewalk at the edge of his yard.

"Lucky," he calls. "Come and see what this boy wants."

A colored kid runs around the house. I recognize him. He's come into the store several times. He calls my mother "Boss Lady," and she thinks he's cute. He's about my age, but he doesn't go to my school. The colored kids have their own schools.

"Whatcha want?" Lucky says.

"You work here?"

"My mama works here. She takes care of Mr. Garza. I'm jest helpin' out."

I glance at the old man, who has placed both hands on the arms of the chair, ready to push himself up if he has to.

"Whatcha want?" Lucky asks again.

"Well it's like this, see. There's a scrap metal drive down at the theater. It's for the war effort, you know? And I was wonderin' if Mr. Garza would let me take in his old jalopy."

"You want his car?" Lucky laughs.

"What's he sayin', boy?" Mr. Garza shouts.

"Jest a minute, sir," Lucky answers.

"You want his car?"

"Well, he can't use it. It's a broken down piece of junk. Doesn't even have tires anymore. It's just sittin' up on blocks. 'Sides, he's too old to drive anyway."

Lucky laughs again. "Don't none of that matter. He ain't gonna give you his jalopy."

I take another look at Mr. Garza. He's lifting himself up, ready to come over. Lucky's right, he'll never give me that car, and Victor's getting heavy. I lower him to the ground and hold onto his hand tight.

"That your brother?" Lucky asks.

"My nephew. My brother's in the war."

"Mine too."

"Really?"

"Sure. Ain't you never heard of the Buffalo soliders? The colored unit? Been around since the Civil War."

"Well, yeah. Just didn't think any of them was from around here."

Victor's tugging on my hand now. "Go, go," he's saying. I let him lead me back down the street. Lucky follows.

"You want scrap? I know where you could get some."

"Where?"

"Near my house. I'd have to show you."

"Why give it to me? Why don't you just turn it in yourself?"

Lucky laughs again. "Somethin' tells me that theater owner don't want no colored kid winnin' his contest. I'll get you the scrap for a cut of the dough."

"I don't know," I say. "I'm already splitting it with my friend. If we cut you in, there won't be much left for us."

"I won't take much," Lucky says. "Jest two of those dollars would do me for now."

Two dollars to Lucky would still leave nine for me and nine for Gary. "How do I know you got anything good?"

"I'll show you. You gotta come to my neighborhood, though."

"How far is your house?"

"Not far. Ten-minute walk."

That's too far to carry Victor, but if this Lucky does have something, it might be worth going.

"Okay," I say. "Meet me in front of the store in five minutes. I've got to get the buggy for Victor."

"You might want to change him while you at it. Looks like he could use it."

I pick up Victor and sure enough, he's soaked through his diaper. His bottom is wet on my arm. I hate that feeling. I'm hoping Abuelita hasn't lain down for her *siesta*, otherwise I'll have to change him myself, and I haven't yet mastered how to hold him down and work the diaper pins at the same time. Abuelita's not sleeping, but she's not home either. She's probably at the church. She goes there every day to pray a rosary for Ernesto.

"Okay, kid," I say. "You can make this hard or you can make this easy."

Victor makes it hard.

By the time I change the baby's diaper and pants and fetch the buggy from the back porch, Lucky is already waiting for me in front of the store.

"Where are you going?" Mamá calls to me.

"Just taking Victor for a walk."

"Come back soon. It's almost time for lunch."

I have to tell Lucky a couple of times to slow down. The buggy has a bad wheel and it wobbles, and Victor keeps trying to climb over the side as we walk.

"Where are we going?" I ask. "To your house?"

Lucky laughs again. "Now what you think I got at

my house? Nothin', that's what."

"Then where are you takin' me?" I ask, noticing that most of the faces I'm passing on this street are black.

"Well, you comin' up on Mr. Garza that way got me thinkin'. There's an old woman lives down the street from me. She got a rusty, ol' push mower sittin' out back, but her yard's gone to weed. Seems to me she got no more use for that mower."

"Is she like Mr. Garza? Will she let you have it?"

"Don't know. But my mama say it never hurts to ask."

When we reach the old woman's house, Lucky holds out his hand to stop me. "You stay here. She was born way back in slavery days. She see a white boy on her property, she gonna 'spect trouble."

Lucky hops up the woman's front steps. Victor is leaning out of the carriage, gripping the tops of her picket fence. He's pulling so hard, the whole fence is shaking. I have to wrestle his hands free, and by that time, Lucky has disappeared inside the house. I wait for several minutes, pushing the buggy up and down the street to keep Victor from climbing out. People are staring at me as they pass, and I wonder now why I had to come along. Why didn't I just send Lucky to get the mower and bring it back? Just about then, he comes around the back of her house, pushing the mower as fast as he can.

"Les go," he says, "'fore she changes her mind."

He's trotting ahead of me with the mower, which is squeaking and squealing, and I'm trying to keep up while the wobbly buggy wheel shudders. We're both laughing as we cut down the alleys on the way back to the store so fewer people will see us. Out back of my house, we stop. "What did she say?" I ask.

"I told her your father was a block warden and he sent us 'round to find scrap for the war effort. When she looked out the winda and saw you was white, she thought she better go along."

"So that's why you took me?"

"Yeah. They's benefits to bein' white."

"Strange to hear you say that. Plenty of Anglos don't think Mexicans are any better than coloreds." I'm thinking of the signs you sometimes see on restaurant windows in the small towns near San Antonio, the ones that say "No Mexicans allowed."

Lucky glances up at the back of my house. "Sure looks like you got it better to me," he says.

Funny, all my life, my family has struggled. So many mouths to feed, so much work to do. We've pinched pennies wherever we could, like this stupid haircut of mine. I never thought of us as having much, but now I look at our house and see what Lucky sees—a sturdy two-story with a fresh coat of paint, a car parked out back, a busy store up front—and I realize it must look like a lot to him.

"Whatcha gonna do with your two dollars?" I ask.

"Teacher say if I'm gonna do better in school this year, I gotta get me some glasses, but Mama needs a bit more to pay for 'em. I told her I could quit school, get a job, but she wouldn't have none of that. Said I got to finish through eighth grade at least. Watcha thinkin' 'bout spending your money on?"

"Haven't made up my mind yet," I say.

Lucky goes to lean the mower against the house.

"No wait," I say. "We can't put it there. One of them Wagner boys might snatch it."

"Where then?"

I look around, and my eyes settle on the Mueller house three doors down. It's boarded up now. As soon as their son enlisted, the Muellers moved to north Texas to run his shoe store while he's at war. They've got a tall, wooden fence around the property. I reach over the top of the gate and unlatch it, letting us in. We put the mower there, and then I go back to the house to bring over the rest of the stuff that Gary and I have been piling on the back porch. Abuelita hasn't liked stepping around it anyway.

"Pretty good stash," Lucky says. "Think you'll win now?"

"Nah. I could, though, if I could get my hands on this one thing I've been wanting."

"Mr. Garza's jalopy?"

"No," I say. "You're right. He'll never give it up. Somethin' else."

"Hope you get it," Lucky says. "Sure could use that money."

"Then find me something else," I say. "If you do, bring it here. You can just unlatch the gate."

Lucky laughs. "Don't think folks would cotton to a colored boy sneakin' onto other people's property. I'll bring it to you. You can put it away."

"Yeah, right," I say. I like this kid, but the Negro kids mostly stick with their own kind.

I reach for Victor, but he starts to run. It takes me a minute to chase him down. I pull him by the sleeve toward the house. I can hear Lucky chuckling as he goes.

7

What No One Wants to Hear

A couple of days later, I'm at the store helping Mamá box up some groceries for Sister Frances and Sister Margaret. Sister Margaret looks faint. Well and why wouldn't she, wearing that long, black, wool habit in this heat?

"Mrs. Montoya," Sister Frances whispers. "Would you mind giving us a ride up the hill in your car?"

"Of course not," Mamá says, but she doesn't sound convincing. Tía Silvia is late, so it's only Abuelo and me in the store with her.

"Shall I run the register while you're gone, Mamá? I think I know how."

"No, *mijo*. Silvia will be here soon, and I'll send Rosa up from the house. Just keep an eye on things for a moment. And sweep up, there by the front door. Those roofers who came in had dirt on their boots."

I sigh and reach for the broom. Several minutes later, Tía Silvia comes dancing into the store. She snatches the broom from my hands and drops it on the ground. Then she grabs my hands and spins me around.

"What are you doing?"

"Carlos is coming home for a visit!" Carlos is her fiancé. He's been up in Detroit working in a war factory since January. "He'll be here tomorrow!"

"That's great, Tía," I say. She's still holding my hands, and it's embarrassing. Rosa is watching us from the cash register now. "Why don't you go tell Juanita," I say to get rid of her. "Maybe you can do something special for Carlos at Abuelo's birthday party."

"Good idea," Tía Silvia says. "You're a sweetie, Miguel." She pulls me forward and kisses me on the head like Mamá does.

As I'm wiping off the kiss, I hear someone snicker. I turn to see Alfonso watching me. Somehow that guy always manages to sneak in at exactly the wrong moment. This time I decide to ignore him. I pick up my broom and turn my back on him as I sweep. I sense him moving and I'm glad, but then I realize he's not moving away from me. He's moving toward me. He taps my shoulder, and there's a hard sadness in his voice. "Looks like you're about to get some news," he says.

I follow his gaze to the front counter. Standing there is a sight no one wants to see in wartime, a Western Union boy. He's holding a telegram and asking for Rosa Montoya. Juanita and Tía Silvia are coming into the store from the back, giggling like schoolgirls, but they stop short when they see the Western Union boy. So does Abuelo, who's been standing in the corner talking to old Mr. Sanchez, the knife sharpener, and Mamá, who has just come back from dropping off the nuns. All of our eyes fix on the telegram in the boy's hand. Since it came for Rosa, it can only be about Ernesto.

Rosa doesn't speak; she meekly holds out her hand. The Western Union boy slips her the telegram, nods solemnly, and backs out of the store. I glance at Alfonso, but he drops his head to the side, avoiding my gaze. Rosa stares at the paper, her tears falling onto the telegram, but she doesn't move. No one does. My heart is pounding. I want someone to open the telegram. I want to know what happened to my brother.

"Here, let me have it," I say.

That seems to snap Mamá to her senses. "No, *mijo*, I'll read it."

She takes the telegram from Rosa's trembling hand, opens it carefully, and reads. Her hand flies to her heart, and she sinks back against the counter. "It says Ernesto is missing in action over France. When they get more details we'll be notified." Juanita is the first to cry. She throws her arms around Rosa, who can't stop shaking her head, her breath coming out in ragged bursts.

"What do they mean 'missing over France?'" I ask, but no one answers. The women have huddled together to reread the telegram, Mamá shushing them so the customers won't overhear. "What do they mean?" I say again, trying to sound more demanding, but Mamá is helping Rosa back to the house, and Juanita is drying her eyes as she takes Rosa's place at the register.

"It means he was shot down over enemy territory in France," Alfonso says.

"Is he okay?"

"No telling. Even if he bailed out in time, there are lots of broken bones in those jumps. Sometimes parachutes get caught in trees."

"But if he bailed out, he might have escaped, right?"

"Doubtful. That area is crawling with Krauts. *If* he survived, he's probably on his way to some German prisoner-of-war camp."

I can tell by the way he says it he doesn't think my brother is alive. But he doesn't know Ernesto. I advance on Alfonso. "Why don't you go home? You don't even have any purchases today. You just hang around here 'cause you've got nothing better to do."

He gives me a hard stare then marches out of the store. He doesn't even glance at Juanita when she mumbles a half-hearted "good afternoon." As soon as he leaves, Juanita slumps back against the shelves, quiet. I'm sure the women have told Abuelita by now, but what about Papá? I'm thinking about going out to find him, but then I remember Victor.

"Where's the baby?" I ask.

"Here."

I lean over the counter and see Victor sitting on a blanket behind the counter, chewing on the ear of his stuffed bunny. Juanita's not paying him any mind. She's staring off across the room, her arms wrapped tightly around her.

"Hand Victor to me."

"Why?"

"It's lunchtime. He's probably hungry. I'll go fix him something."

Juanita nods, but she doesn't move. I push past her and scoop up Victor. He squawks at me loudly until I promise him some peaches for lunch. He loves peaches, just like Ernesto did—I mean does. I bet there are no peaches in a prison camp. I wonder if there's much food at all. I talk to Victor as I cross the yard. I need to hear myself say things out loud. "Don't worry about your daddy, Victor. He'll be fine. Tough as nails. No dang Nazi could ever get the best of him. We'll get you something to eat, then we'll go look for Papá. He should be finishing up his deliveries soon."

The roar of an engine drowns out my words. Victor tips his head way back, making it harder to carry his weight. I stop, and we watch it fly over.

"P-38," I say out of habit . . . and I try not to cry.

That night after supper, it's too quiet in my house. Not even Abuelo can think of anything to say. I get permission to run down to Gary's. He's probably heard about Ernesto already—news travels fast in this neighborhood. I scoot around back of Gary's house and knock on the screen door off the kitchen. When no one answers, I open the door and call in. Gary's mother appears from the dining room, supper dishes in her hands. Her face softens. "Oh hello, Miguel," she says. "Gary's up in his room. Go on up, dear." Mrs.

Bauer never calls me "dear." I wonder if she knows.

I take the stairs two at a time to Gary's room. It's hotter upstairs than it is down, and I wonder why he wants to be cooped up in his room in this heat. But I don't wonder for long. Gary's sitting at his desk, bent over a new model airplane. He barely hears me come in. "Oh wow," I say. "Where'd you get that?"

"My grandmother. It's an early birthday present, and she wanted to thank me for weeding her garden the last time we visited. She shouldn't have thanked me. I didn't even want to do it. Ma made me."

"What model is it?"

"P-47 Thunderbolt. It's just out!"

Gary's room is a shrine to aviation. He's cut out ads for model airplanes and hung them on his wall along with old covers from magazines like *Life* and *Popular Aviation*. Anything that shows an airplane or a pilot. His flying helmet and goggles dangle from one bed post, his bomber jacket from the other. His larger model planes hang from his ceiling. The rest are lined up along shelves on his walls, the top of his bureau, the lid to his old toy box. They sit on the floor by the head of his bed. He's even saved every box from every kit he's ever assembled. There are so many of them now that they peek out from under his bed. I pick up the plans to the plane that are lying on his bed and study them for a moment, but I don't have the patience for model airplanes. Unfortunately, Gary does. He'll sit there for hours when he gets a new plane. I might as well go home.

But then something catches my eye. It's sitting on top of his bureau. It's the piece of wing from the airplane that crashed in our neighborhood. He has it sitting up there among his model planes and the toy planes from his childhood, like some favored souvenir. Something in me stirs, and I drop the plans. I cross the room and pick up the piece of wing, and when I do, I feel myself getting hotter. "You kept this?" I accuse.

Gary looks up from the propeller he's about to affix to the nose. "Why wouldn't I? It's cool."

"What's cool about a plane crash, Gary?"

"You didn't mind it when I showed it to you before."

"But things are different now. You should put it on the scrap pile."

"Why? What's eating you?"

"Didn't your mother tell you?"

"Tell me what?" He's standing now.

"Ernesto was shot down. He's MIA." I drop down on the bed.

"Oh I didn't know," Gary says with a low, dull whistle. He sets his model plane down carefully and joins me on the bed.

"When did you find out?"

"This afternoon. Western Union boy came."

"That's tough, Miguel. So . . . do you think he's . . . dead?"

I glare at him. "Of course not. Probably got picked up by the Krauts. The Red Cross will find him. They'll let us know where he is soon."

Gary picks up the plans and traces a line with his finger.

"What're you doing?"

"Just checking something."

"Didn't you hear what I said?"

"Yeah, I heard. I mean I'm sorry about Ernesto and all, but there's nothin' I can do right?"

"You can forget about your crummy plane for a minute. You could put that wing piece from the wreck on the scrap pile."

"Why? Getting rid of it won't help your brother."

"It's bad luck keeping it. And it doesn't seem right. Men died in that crash."

Gary frowns. "But it's the only piece of a real plane I've got. Just don't think about where it came from."

I jump up. "How am I supposed to do that? You saying you're really gonna keep it? After everything I said?"

Gary sits back at his desk and picks up the model again, and I know he's made up his mind.

"Fine," I say. "Keep your stupid piece of plane. But I don't want your help with the scrap contest."

"Well, half of that junk is mine."

"So come and get it. See if I care." I stomp out of his room and thunder down the stairs. Mrs. Bauer looks up from washing dishes. "Miguel, what's wrong?" she asks, but I bolt past her and out the back door.

When I get home, I dart up to my room to grab my yo-yo, but as I reach the landing, Mamá calls up the stairs for me to be quiet, and I quickly understand why. Victor is asleep in his crib, his head damp with sweat. Rosa must have put him down early and gone to bed herself. I can hear her crying softly through her door. I grab my yo-yo off my nightstand and warm up with The Sleeper. I don't worry about waking Victor. That kid could sleep though a bombing raid.

Ernesto gave me this yo-yo for my eighth birthday. Before he left for the war, I'd gotten pretty good. I could do Around the World and Rock the Cradle, but I was never as good as Ernesto. I haven't played with my yo-yo much since he left, and playing with it now makes me feel sad. I pick up the photograph of my brother in his flight suit and lie down on my bed. I never sleep in this room in the summer. It's too hot. I've got a little bed outside on the sleeping porch. But I'm not ready to go out there by myself yet. The fan in the corner rustles my clothes, and I try to remember what it was like when Ernesto shared this room with me, a long time ago when I was Victor's age and Ernesto was mine. But I can't remember. I can only remember him older, teaching me yo-yo tricks, showing me how to put sawdust on the store floors at night, marrying Rosa.

I wish I were old enough to enlist. I'd learn to fly like Ernesto and bomb the heck out of those Nazis. I'd get my brother back. But the war will probably be over before I'm old enough to fight, and there's nothing I can do about it. I throw the yo-yo against the wall, and Victor stirs. I lean over the crib and rub his back till he settles down again, his long eyelashes resting on his chubby cheeks. I remember the promise I made to Ernesto in my letter about Victor. I know he wouldn't have gotten that letter before he got shot down, but I wish he had. Wherever he is, I'd like for him to know there's at least something I can do for him. I can watch out for Victor the way he always watched out for me. I turn suddenly, looking for my yo-yo, afraid it might have broken, but it's fine. I roll up the string and set the yo-yo carefully on my nightstand next to the picture of my brother.

8

No Heroes in War Time

It's been over a week since we got word about Ernesto, but we still think about him every hour of every day. Mr. Sanchez said it might be two months before we learn something more. That's how long it took him to hear about his son. So we'll hurry up and wait. That's all.

School starts in just over a week, and the Empire's scrap metal contest ends on Saturday. I haven't made much progress finding more scrap, not even with Lucky's help, although Mrs. Hernandez gave up one of her mother's big chili pots, and Lucky's mother talked Mr. Garza into donating an old brass headboard from a bed that hadn't been used in thirty years. Even still, it won't be enough to beat Tug Wagner. I've pretty much given up on the contest. Haven't been in the mood for it anyway. A silly scrap metal contest isn't going to do much to end the war and bring my brother home.

Gary never came to get his share of the scrap, but he hasn't come by to talk to me either. Alejandro says Gary went to visit his grandmother for a while. It's pretty boring around here without Gary. Alejandro and I got the kite up for a minute the other day. I was right, the tail was too heavy, but the weather hasn't been good for kite flying lately, the air so thick with heat and humidity and the breeze absent. It's early in the day, and my chores are already done. Rosa took Victor to the doctor for a check-up, so there's nothing to do. I'm leaning on the counter, playing with my yo-yo and eyeing the walk-in cooler where we store the milk and eggs and meat, wondering if I could sneak in there for a minute to cool off, but Mamá hates it when I open the door for no reason. It lets the cold air out, she complains. But it sure feels good in there.

All of a sudden, I hear a commotion out on the street, and I rush to the front door. Outside, I see a parade of people behind a truck, the meat truck! They're laughing and running along behind it. Some of them wave to me, and I wave back. We've always sold a lot of meat at our store, so the ration board allows us a higher allotment. When the meat truck arrives, people come from all over the neighborhood to be the first to get the best cuts. I glance to the back of the store and see our two butchers straighten their hats and tighten their long aprons. It'll be busy in the store soon. "Move away from the counter," Juanita orders. "I don't want you getting in the way."

"What do you expect me to do?"

"I don't know. Go clean your room."

"Clean your own room! You've got so many clothes in your closet you can't even shut the door."

"Oh be quiet, Miguel. You're such a child."

To prove her point, I stick my tongue out at her and get the reaction I'd hoped for. Her eyes flash and she reaches for me, but I sidestep her hand, laughing. I back toward the door, making faces at her as I go, and almost run into Lucky, who is standing inside the doorway.

"Hiya, Luck. Whatcha doin' here?"

"I come to see if you wanted to look for scrap."

"Ah, what's the use? The contest is in a few days. We've got no chance."

"Well there's nothin' else to do."

He's got a point there. "Get out of the doorway, you two," my sister yells, and I scrunch up my face at her again.

"Hey, I've got an idea," I say. "Come with me."

We dash through the store and out the back toward my house. Lucky hesitates on the porch steps. "It's okay, follow me."

"What're we doin'?"

"I told you, I've got an idea."

We pass Abuelita in the kitchen, but she pays us no mind. We dart up the stairs, and I check every bedroom, but no one else is home. I move across Juanita's room straight to her closet. "What're you doin'?" Lucky asks.

"Well it's like this, see. Juanita never throws anything away. She's got clothes in here she hasn't worn in years. She'll never even notice if we borrow a few buckles or metal buttons for the war effort. In fact, I think she even has a woman's suit that has a zipper."

"If you takin' things, I bes' be goin.'"

"Nah, trust me, she'll never even notice. Here, take the buttons off this coat. There's not much use for a coat this warm in San Antonio anyway."

"No, sir," Lucky says. "I ain't touchin' nothin.'"

"Okay, then, you be the lookout. Stand at the door and tell me if anyone is coming."

Lucky frowns, but he goes to the door.

"Hey," I say. "Look at all these shoes! Some of 'em

have rubber heels. I bet I could pry a few off."

"But the contest is for scrap metal this time."

"Yeah, but you know they'll have a rubber matinee soon."

"Boy, you gonna get yourself in some trouble," Lucky says, but there's a hint of a smile on his lips.

I make sure to hang the clothes I've "borrowed" from in the back of the walk-in closet, and I hide the heelless shoes under a shelf. Now that the job is done, I have a twinge of guilt, but I tell myself that by the time Juanita notices what's missing, the war might be over, and then she can easily buy new buttons and buckles. I pick up all my treasures off the floor and make a pouch out of the front of my shirt. I fold it closed so no one will see, and Lucky and I sneak out back to the Mueller's house, open the gate, and deposit our loot in the spittoon that the Sisters provided.

"It don't amount to much weight," Lucky says.

"Yeah, but it was fun." I chuck him on the shoulder and we head out, latching the gate behind us, and then the truth of our situation hits home again. There's still a long summer day stretching ahead of us with nothing to do. We sit down with our backs to the fence and our legs crossed, looking up at the sky. "B-29," I say as the heavy bomber roars over, headed for Kelly Field.

"You like planes, huh?"

"Yeah, don't you?"

"Planes is fine. I like the big ships myself. Firing them big guns, like they do in the newsreels. Bein' out on the ocean. Course, they don't let coloreds do much on the ships 'cept be a cook or a steward. I'd do it, though, if I was older."

"Wouldn't you want to be a soldier like your brother?"

"Soldiering is fine, but them big ships jest call to me."

"Miguel?" I hear my mother holler. I jump to my feet. "I gotta go."

"If I find anythin' else, I'll bring it to the store."

"Look, Lucky," I say, turning back to him. "It's like I said. We've got no chance of winning. You might as well go home."

Mamá is waiting for me on the back porch. She's holding Victor. "Rosa is back, and I need her help in the store. You watch the baby."

I sigh and reach out my hands for him, but I don't complain. I've been trying not to complain since we got the word about Ernesto. Mamá and

Rosa have enough to worry about. I lug Victor around the house and through the back door of the store. I'm curious to see the commotion. There's a long line still at the butcher counter, and the store is filled with people. Victor bends over, reaching for the ground. I set him down but hold his hand firmly. He doesn't like that one bit. He pulls me toward the front of the store.

"Where are we goin', Little V?" I ask. He drags me through the store to the front counter and points to the shelf where we keep the candy. He's recently discovered it, and now he wants candy all the time. As I'm struggling to pull and then coax him away from the candy shelf, I catch sight of Alfonso standing by the fruit bins. He's picking up produce with his one hand and pretending to inspect it, but his eyes are somewhere else. They're watching my sister, who is ringing up a customer. She casts him a shy smile. It's not like Juanita to act bashful. I grin. "Come on, Little V." I pick up my squirming nephew and cross the store. Alfonso sees me coming. He surprises me again by reaching out a finger to tickle Victor under the chin.

"At least now I know why you hang around here so much," I say. "Why don't you go talk to her?"

"Who?"

"Oh don't play wise with me. You like my sister."

"Sure, I like her. She's a nice girl."

"No, I mean you really like her. Why don't you ask her out?"

Alfonso's eyes grow dark. "Do you really think a girl like that would go out with a broken-down bum like me?"

"There you go again. Why you gotta be like that?"

"Listen kid, you don't know nothin' about me. You understand?"

"I know you lost your arm in the war and you're sore about it. I know you got no job, and you live alone, and you sit in your car wishing you were somebody else. I know you won't give me your fence even though it could help me win the contest. Heck, it could help us win the war! But I guess you don't care about that anymore. You only care about yourself."

Alfonso grabs me by the arm and yanks me and Victor toward the front door. "What're you doing?" Juanita asks, stepping forward, but he brushes past her, still jerking me along. He drags me to the end of the block and down an alley. He backs me up against the outer wall of a tailor's shop and paces back and forth, running his hand through his thick, brown hair and shaking all over. He stops in front of me and says, "You think I'm supposed to act like some sort of hero, don't you? You think your brother's a hero—"

"My brother *is* a hero."

"No, he's not. There are no heroes in wartime, kid. Just a bunch of men trying not to get killed so they can come home. You know how I lost this arm? Not in some daring charge on the enemy. I didn't lose it taking a bunch of prisoners single-handedly. I didn't even lose it in battle. I lost it during a march. One of our own men tripped over a tree root and accidentally shot me in the arm. He was just a kid, seventeen, from some city back East. Had never even held a gun till he joined up. And that's all it took. A moment of carelessness, and I was out of the war. And now what? Who's gonna hire a one-armed man? How am I gonna provide for a wife and family now? I can't even hold onto my own house."

Victor is chewing on his fingers, his head on my shoulder. There are tears in his eyes, but he doesn't cry. I pat his back to soothe him. I should probably take him away from here, get him some candy in the store, but Alfonso has sat down against the wall beside me and I'm looking down on him, and from this angle, he doesn't look so tough. He looks mostly scared and sad. I lower myself down beside him, Victor still in my arms.

"What do you mean you can't hold onto your house, Alfonso?"

He drops his head back against the wall. "It was left to me by my father. He died a few months ago. My mother has been dead for years. Papá had been sick, but he hadn't told me he couldn't make the house payments. I guess he didn't want to worry me while I was in the service. I owe too much in back payments now. The bank is taking the house."

"Is that why you couldn't give me the fence?"

He laughs that hard, sharp laugh of his. "You and that fence. Yes, Miguel, that's why. It's not my house anymore."

Victor is whining now, pointing toward Clark Avenue. He wants to go home. "How much do you owe?" I ask.

"Enough."

"Maybe I can help you find a job. You could ask the bank for more time."

"I told you, there are no jobs for me. Not even the nuns would hire me. I thought I could do some yard work for them or some fix-it jobs, but they've got a man for that. They offered to help me, but I won't take charity."

"There must be something you can do."

He stands up. "I told you, there's nothing. You still don't get it, do you? What did I expect? You're just a kid. Go on back to the store. I won't come around bothering you anymore." He puts his one hand in his pocket and slumps off down the street. As soon as he's gone, Victor wants down. He's not afraid anymore. But I am. There was something in Alfonso's eyes that worries me.

I walk Victor back to the store, and Juanita rushes over to us. "What was that all about? Where did he take you?"

"Nowhere. He just wanted to talk."

"Talk? That didn't look like he wanted to talk. Did you say something to upset him?"

"No!"

"He used to be such a nice guy in high school. I used to think he liked me. But you're right. He is an odd duck. Maybe you should stay away from him, Miguel."

"He's still a nice guy, Juanita. You don't have to high-hat him just 'cause he's down on his luck. And he does like you, but that's only because he doesn't know you. Come on, Victor. Let's get Abuelita to change your diaper." I stalk off toward the house with my smelly nephew in tow, my sister shaking her head as she watches me go. For the first time all summer, I'm actually looking forward to the start of school. It'll be nice to be away from the grown-ups all day. Even the nuns are easier to take than my sister.

9

The Knife Grinder's News

Today is Abuelo's birthday. He's seventy years old, and we're having a *fiesta* to celebrate. Abuelo thought we should cancel the party. He said it might not be right to be festive when we still haven't heard about Ernesto, but Mamá insisted. She said it would do us all some good to get our minds off our troubles for a night. Abuelita must agree. She's been humming *"Paso del Norte"* all morning. Abuelita never remembers the words to those old Mexican songs. I've tried to teach her, but the words never stick, and eventually she swats me away like a fly. She hands me the sweeper and tells me to go over the rug in the parlor again, though I've done it once already. Everyone will stay in the backyard because of the heat, but Abuelita wants the house spotless anyway. You'd think the King of Spain was coming for a visit.

This morning Papá and I strung paper streamers from the back porch to the trees at the edge of our yard. We took one of the *piñatas* from the front window of the store and hung it from a high branch for the children. We carried the dining room table and a smaller side table into the yard and covered them with Mamá's best tablecloths. Juanita picked a few lilies from the flower bed near the house for one table and made paper flowers for the other. All of my aunts, uncles, and cousins and several of our family's friends will be here tonight. As I'm finishing up the rug, I hear the high ring of a bell outside. It can only be Mr. Sanchez, the knife sharpener. He comes by every month or two to sharpen our knives and scissors. Here's my chance to get out of the housework.

"Abuelita, Mr. Sanchez is here. You better let me take the knives out. You wouldn't want them dull for the *fiesta.*"

Abuelita shakes her head at me, but she picks out two knives and digs a few coins out of a Mason jar in the cupboard. I carry the knives and the money out front, where Mr. Sanchez is sitting on his bike. It's not just any bike, though. He's got a stand that holds the rear wheel in place, and when he pedals, a belt turns the grinding wheels that are mounted on a shaft on the handlebars. He takes one of my knives, holds it to the grinding wheel, and starts pedaling.

"This sure is a swell bike, Mr. Sanchez."

"Yep. Alfonso rigged it up for me."

"Alfonso Rivera?"

"The very same. He used to help me out before the war. Smart as a whip, that boy. Real whiz with numbers. I used to tell him he should go to college, become an engineer, but then the war started and he joined up."

"Have you seen him since he came home, Mr. Sanchez? You know about his arm?"

"Yeah, I know. I rang by his house a couple of weeks ago to see if he needed any grinding. He asked about my son, and we talked a bit about the war." Mr. Sanchez leans into his work, and the knife sparks a little.

"Did Alfonso tell you what he did during the war, sir?"

"Oh sure. Alfonso was a medic. Not many men braver than the medics. I suspect he saved quite a few lives during the Battle of Guadalcanal. Some pretty fierce fighting there, and it sounds like he might have pulled more than a few men to safety."

"So he *was* a hero."

"I suppose so. But he'd never think of himself that

way. Not Alfonso." Mr. Sanchez tests the sharpness of the blade with his thumb and hands it back to me.

I get the light of an idea. "Maybe you could hire him again, Mr. Sanchez. He sure could use the work. The bank is about to take his house."

Mr. Sanchez raises an eyebrow. "I'm sure sorry to hear that. But I never did pay Alfonso. He just helped me out. Not much money to be made grinding knives, son."

"There must be something we can do. Maybe if we went and talked to the bank."

"Whoa now, boy. You shouldn't go meddling in other people's affairs. A man's got to solve his own problems. Alfonso will figure something out. Like I told you, he's a smart boy."

Mr. Sanchez hands me back the last knife and kicks up the stand on his bike.

I drop down on the porch steps and listen to the sound of his bell as he moves up the street. I don't understand grown-ups sometimes. They act all sorry for other people's misfortunes, but they don't step in to help. And they tell us kids to stay out of things too.

As I'm stewing about that, I see Gary coming up the walk, a huge burlap sack slung over his shoulder.

"What're you doing here?"

"Ah gee, Miguel. You still sore? I brought this over for the scrap pile. My grandma gave it to us."

"I thought you wanted to take your half."

"I never said that, you did. You still want to win, don't ya?"

"Course I want to win." I can't resist my curiosity now. "So what'd she give ya?"

Gary beams and turns the sack upside down. Out topples a tea kettle, a coal bucket, and an old gasoline can.

"That's worth a few pounds right there!" I say.

"Yeah, ain't it great?"

"Let's put it with the rest." We scoop up our loot and rush across the lawn to the Mueller's. When we unlatch the fence, Gary whistles a high, shrill whistle. "Look at the brass headboard! Where'd you get that?"

"Mr. Garza."

"That's swell."

"Hey Gary, we're having a party tonight. All my cousins will be here. You wanna come?"

"Sure."

"Good. Come at seven o'clock. You can bring Alejandro if you want. We can get up a game of baseball at Mr. Garza's. Can you bring your bat?"

"That the only reason you're inviting me?"

103

"Nah, of course not," I say, blushing. It's not the *only* reason, but it's one reason. Gary's the only kid I know with a decent bat. The rest of us use sticks. But he lost his baseball a year ago, so we always use mine. Neither one of us owns a mitt, but that's okay. Most of the kids on the block just use their hands.

At that moment, we hear the excited squeals of Silvia and Juanita coming from the house. "Must be Carlos," I explain. "Silvia's boyfriend. He's home for a visit. I should go."

Gary nods. "See you tonight then."

Abuelo has stepped onto the porch, looking for me no doubt, or trying to escape the giddiness inside the house. He waves me over to the table and chairs on the porch and we sit. He fans himself with his hat, and I search for something to say. "So . . . how does it feel to be seventy?"

Abuelo gives me a sidelong look. "I was a boy myself once, you know? I haven't always been an old man."

"You're not old, Abuelo. Abuelita says you're still strong as an ox."

Abuelo's eyes light up. "Let's see if that's true." He takes off his jacket and props his elbow on the wooden table. He tosses me a grin and waits for me to take his hand. Within a few seconds, he's pinned my arm to the table. I've never won an arm wrestling match with Abuelo, and I guess I never will.

He stands and dons his jacket again. "We should get back inside, say hello to Carlos. He'll be marrying your aunt soon, you know? Then she'll move up north with him."

"Can I run the cash register *then*, Abuelo?"

Abuelo chuckles and rubs my head. "We'll see, *mijo*. We'll see."

10

The Trouble Begins

Though it's late in the evening, as soon as Mr. Garza hears the first crack of the bat, he comes shuffling out his door and drags his chair to the middle of the yard to keep an eye on us kids. Lucky comes out with him.

"Whatcha doin' here so late?" I ask Lucky.

"I been spending the last couple of nights here. The old man has a cough, and Mamá's worried about him." As if on cue, Mr. Garza doubles over in a coughing fit. Lucky pats his back hard. Mr. Garza wipes his mouth on a handkerchief and pushes Lucky away. Lucky just laughs.

Between my cousins, Gary, Alejandro, and me, we've got enough kids to play if a few play on both sides, but then who should come up the walk but the Wagner boys. "Looks like you got room for a few more," says Tug.

I glance at Gary, and he shakes his head slightly. Alejandro does too. As I'm trying to figure out how to get rid of them, one of my cousins pipes up, "Sure, come on." He doesn't know the Wagner boys, so he can't imagine what we're in for, but before I can say any more, Tug snatches the bat. "I'm up," he announces, and everyone scoots back to their positions.

I'm pitching, and it's not too hard to size up Tug. He's gonna hit the ball and hit it hard. He's waggling the bat, waiting for my pitch, and I'm wondering if I can get away with walking him or if that would make him mad. To find out, I throw a lousy fastball that veers off to the left. He drops the bat and stalks right toward me. "Is that the best you got?"

"Nah, the sun got in my eyes, that's all."

"Well, you better get it right this time or else." He leans over me, and I sink down in my shoes. My older cousin comes off third base to help me, but I shake my head, and he steps back to his position.

Tug returns to home plate and picks up the bat. He spits on the street and waggles the bat again. I sigh and let the ball fly. He has to step into the pitch, but he hits it. A pop fly to left field. I hold my breath, willing Gary not to catch it, but Gary knows better. He lets the ball bounce a couple of times then scoops it up and tosses it to first, but Tug is already safely on base.

Tug's brother is next up to bat. And that's how the game goes for a while, all of us playing our best unless one of the Wagner boys is up to bat. And none of us protest when Tug takes over the pitcher's mound. It's easier to let him have his way, and it doesn't hurt too much when his balls bean us on the leg or shoulder. I'm never quite sure if he's just a bad throw or if he's trying to hit us. Tug's team pulls ahead six to four. "Get used to losin," Tug says as my team takes the field. "I've got that scrap contest all wrapped up."

"That's what you think," Gary says. "We've got a pretty good stash going. We've even got a brass headboard."

"That so?" Tug says. "Keeping it at your place, huh, Miguel?"

"Wouldn't you like to know?"

Tug nudges his brother, and they walk off the field.

I turn on Gary. "What'd you tell him that for?"

"Well, you said yourself we could still win. Besides, I didn't say where it was."

"How hard do you think it's gonna be to figure out where? Now he knows we found a place big enough to put a headboard."

Gary's face goes ashen. "You don't think he'd really steal our stuff, do you?"

"In the shake of a dog's tail."

"Oh . . . I'm sorry, Miguel."

"Hey, sissies," Tug yells. He's up to bat again. "You gonna play or stand around gossiping like a bunch of old hens?"

"Never mind, Gary. Get back in the outfield. We'll have my cousins help us move it later. It'll be fine," I say.

"Move it where?" Gary looks so sorry that it's hard to be mad at him.

"I don't know, my room."

"Will your mother let us?"

"We'll do it while she's busy cleaning up. It's only for a few days."

"Hey, you hear me?" Tug yells. He's dropped the bat and is heading our way. I jerk my head toward the outfield, and Gary runs back. Tug stops and puffs his chest up like the big man he imagines himself to be. I try to throw a good pitch to calm him down, but I'm so distracted worrying about the scrap heap that my pitch drops low and outside. Tug tries to hit it anyway, but the ball catches on the tip of his bat and sails up backward into Mr. Garza's yard. Mr. Garza's eyes fly open. He struggles to rise, but Lucky pats him on the shoulder and runs for the ball. He picks it up, and instead of tossing it to Alejandro, who's playing catcher, he throws the ball all the way back to me. And it's a beauty of a throw. Hard and fast and right to me. I catch it and toss a nod of approval at him. Tug, though, charges over to Lucky, bat in hand. "Keep your hands off the ball," he orders. Lucky takes a few steps back and lowers his head.

"Hey," I call. "It's my ball. I'll say who can touch it."

Tug whirls on me. "You'd let some colored kid play with you?"

At that moment, I notice Tug's big mistake. He's taken a few steps onto Mr. Garza's lawn. All I have to do is stall for a minute, and Mr. Garza will do the rest. "He's not playing with us. He just threw the ball back," I say, watching Mr. Garza shuffle across the yard. Faster than I would have thought possible, the old man yanks the bat out of Tug's hand and shakes it in his face.

"You stay off my property, you here. Go on now, git!" And this time it's Tug who steps back.

There's something so funny about seeing old Mr. Garza advancing on Tug that we all crack up. Tug's face reddens, and he turns on us in a rage.

"You wouldn't catch me playin' with that ball now. Not after *he* touched it. You play a sissy game anyway. My sisters could play better than you."

He calls to his brother, and the two of them stalk off up the street with the sound of our laughter nipping at their heels.

I notice, though, that Lucky isn't laughing. He helps Mr. Garza back to his chair, but he won't look at me. It's only then that I realize I never did ask him if he wanted to play. I open my mouth to say something, but my cousin asks if we can go back to the *fiesta* for a while, and it's easier to walk away than to figure out what to say to Lucky. I'm not feeling too good about it, though, and it doesn't help when Gary sidles up to me and says, "That was pretty brave of you standing up to Tug that way. Why'd you do it?"

"I don't know. Just didn't like the way he was bossing us around."

I don't want to talk about it anymore, so I jog ahead of Gary. I'm still mad about the way the game turned out, still feeling strange about Lucky. I just want to get back to the party and have some fun. That's what this night was supposed to be about, after all.

When we get back to our house, Carlos has borrowed a guitar, and he's singing an old folk song. Abuelo is singing along with him. Abuelita has her eyes closed, and I wonder if the music is taking her back to her younger days in Mexico. Victor and the little kids are toddling around. Some of the younger girls are holding their hands to help them dance, but Victor will have none of that. He does his own funny step, raising first one leg and then the other until he loses his balance and topples over. Rosa reaches down to brush off his hands and help him up. She gives him a huge kiss on the cheek. He squeals and pulls away from her. I grab Gary and lead him toward the food table. Most of the supper food—the *tamales*, the *picadillo*, the *pozole*—is all gone, and there are only a few pieces of cake left. I'm about to dish up when my mother approaches. "Go and find your father, Miguel. Tell him to come back and enjoy the party."

"But Mamá, I was about to get some cake." Abuelita used up what was left of our sugar ration on that cake. There won't be any sugar in our house for a few weeks now.

"I'll get you some. And some for Gary too. But find your father first."

My mouth waters as I watch her cut a sliver of cake. "Where is he, Mamá?"

"At the store. He remembered something he needed to check."

I hurry around the house and through the back door of the store. I find my father there working in the dim light of a kerosene lamp. He's got the accounting books open and is checking the figures. "Papá, Mamá wants you back at the party."

"*Un momento*, Miguel. I couldn't get the books to balance this morning. It's been weighing on me all day."

I realize he's not going to come quickly, and Mamá won't want me returning without him. But my cake is waiting, and I can all but taste it. I look over my father's shoulder at the numbers scratched in the ledger, thinking maybe I can help, but math has never been my best subject. "Do you want me to get you some cake?" I offer, thinking then I can bring my own piece back and eat it.

"No thank you. I already had some. Did you boys finish your game?"

"I guess so."

"You don't sound too happy."

"I'm just out of sorts about this scrap contest. I

114

really wanted to win."

"Still hoping to get that bike, huh?"

"Actually, I was thinking about giving the money to a friend now. He's got some pretty big problems, and I thought the money might help," I say, pulling up an old orange crate to sit on.

"*Sí,*" Papá says, but I'm not sure he really hears me. He's smoothing his thick moustache as he tries to work out a problem, and all of a sudden, I get one of my brilliant ideas. I wonder why I didn't think of it before. But if I don't say it just right, I'll never get him to listen.

"You've been working awfully hard lately," I start.

"Guess we all have," Papá says absently.

"Yeah, with you doing all the deliveries now and unloading the trucks and helping the butchers. Not to mention taking care of the books and all the extra work with the ration points. Seems like more than one man can handle."

"Well, we've always worked hard," Papá says.

"Yeah, but Mamá looks so tired lately. Don't you think she looks tired?"

At this, Papá finally glances up at me. "You think so?"

"Oh she'd never admit it, but I think she could

use a break. I don't think she sleeps well these days, what with all the worry and the work at the store."

Papá leans back in his chair. He's wising up to me. "You got something to say, *mijo*, spit it out."

"How about you let Alfonso Rivera do the books?"

"Alfonso?"

"Yeah, the solider with the missing arm who's been hanging around the store lately. I hear he's really good with numbers, and you don't need two arms to keep a register."

Papá sets his pencil down and studies me. "Is that the friend you were talking about helping?"

"Yeah."

"And did he ask you to ask me?"

I'm startled that he would think this. "Of course not. He'd never want you to know he needs the work. He's too proud."

"Needs the work, huh?"

And that's when I blurt out the whole story. "They're gonna take his house, Papá. But maybe if he could show them he had a job, they'd give him more time. Maybe you could talk to them. They'd listen to you."

"Hold on now, Miguel."

"Please, Papá. He's a war hero. For Ernesto's sake, we oughta help him."

My father's face softens. He rubs his eyes. "Well, I suppose since I'm not paying wages for the delivery boys anymore I could afford to pay a bookkeeper. Mind you, though, I can only give him an hour or two a day. It won't be enough to pay off that debt of his."

"That's okay, Papá. Once people hear he's working for you, maybe some of the other shopkeepers will hire him too. I could even go around and ask them."

"Hang on now, *mijo*. I can't let you bother our neighbors."

"Oh I won't bother anyone, you'll see. Thanks, Papá," I say before he can change his mind. "I'm going to go tell Alfonso right now."

But as I scoot the orange crate back, we hear a loud scream from the back of our house. We rush from the store into the yard. The first thing I see is everyone huddled in a tight circle, the mothers holding the babies up out of the way. Something's on the ground and everyone is looking down on it. It's not until I get closer that I see it's Abuelo. He's lying so still and his skin looks so pale that I'm not sure at first he's alive, but then I see his chest rise beneath his suit jacket. Abuelita is sitting next to him on the ground, squeezing his hand. Mamá is cradling his head in her lap.

"What happened?" I ask Juanita.

"I don't know. He just collapsed."

Tía Silvia races out of the house with a damp cloth and places it on Abuelo's forehead. "I called for an ambulance," she says, and the way my heart is racing, I don't know how she can sound so calm.

Mamá reaches her hand toward me, but I can't move at first. All I can do is stare at my grandfather. My tall, proud grandfather looking up at the sky with the light in his eyes now dimmed. I take Mamá's hand and let her pull me down beside her.

"Will he be all right, Mamá?"

Mamá doesn't answer. She glances at Papá, who is holding Abuelita in his arms. Her head is resting on Papá's shoulder, and she's crying softly. "I'm sure he'll be fine," Papá says to everyone, not just me.

I lean down and whisper in my grandfather's ear. "Did you hear that, Abuelo? You're going to be fine. You're as strong as an ox, remember? And you have to be here when Ernesto comes home. You have to."

The wail of the ambulance comes closer.

11

The Echo of a Cry

I sleep at the kitchen table all night waiting for the phone to ring, but Mamá doesn't call until early in the morning. "How is he?" I fairly scream into the phone. "Is he all right? Will he be home soon? Can I come to see him?"

Rosa and Juanita arrive in the kitchen, and Juanita tries to take the phone from me, but I grip it firmly with both hands and relay to them what Mamá is saying. "The doctors think Abuelo's heart is weak, but he'll be okay if he takes it easy. They want to keep him at the hospital for a few days. Mamá, Abuelita, and Tía Silvia are still at the hospital, but Papá is on his way home to start deliveries."

"Tell her not to worry," Rosa says.

"Don't worry, Mamá," I say into the phone. "We'll handle everything." I hang up, and for a minute we stare at each other as relief washes over us. "Juanita, you should get some breakfast going. Papá will be hungry," I say. She glares at me but moves toward the stove.

I race to the store to start getting things ready. I set out the accounting ledgers for Papá and turn on the lights and sweep up the sawdust from the night before. I turn on the electric fans and dust off the front counter. I'm moving faster than I ever have. Juanita comes in. "I'll open the store," she says importantly, dangling the keys in her hand. The early shoppers are already outside. After a few minutes, Rosa arrives from the house, carrying Victor. She glances around the store nervously. "Is it busy?"

"Not too bad," Juanita responds.

"Your mother wants me to bring a change of clothes for her and Abuelita. Do you think you could manage here for a few minutes without me?"

I start to answer, but Juanita pushes me aside. "Of course we can. Miguel can help the customers and box the groceries, and I'll work the register. We'll be fine."

Rosa doesn't look so sure. "What about Victor? Can you manage him too? They don't like babies in the hospital."

"Give him to me," Juanita says. "I'll keep him behind the counter."

"All right. I'll be right back."

"Don't hurry. We'll be fine," Juanita coos. "Give Abuelo our love."

I can guess what's coming next—a slew of orders from my sister. "All right, Miguel. You stay by my side. Don't go wandering off. That way if I need you to run for more change or to fetch something from the cooler, you'll be available. And try not to talk to me. I have to concentrate."

"Why would I want to talk to you?" I say. "And I know what needs to be done. You don't have to tell me."

She reaches out and grabs my ear. "You better behave, Miguel. I mean it."

She glances up as a customer approaches the counter, eyeing us suspiciously. "I couldn't find the Spam," the woman says. "Are you out?"

"Oh I'm sure not, ma'am. We always keep a well-stocked store. I'll send my brother to the back to find some for you."

I groan as I hustle back to the storage room and find a crate of Spam. I open it and remove a tin of the pink meat and hurry back up front, where Juanita is making polite conversation with the impatient customer. Victor is tugging at Juanita's skirt. He wants candy. Putting him behind the counter isn't such a great idea anymore.

"Miguel, take the baby," Juanita says, handing the Spam to the woman.

"What do you want me to do with him?"

"I don't know. Take him away from the counter. Find him something to play with."

I carry Victor to the front window and interest him in the people walking by. "See that lady with the red hat, Victor? See her hat? Can you say hat? Say hat."

"Hat," he says, patting his head with both hands.

"That's right!" I glance over my shoulder at my sister, who's waiting calmly on a new customer, then turn back toward the window.

"Look, Victor. It's Alfonso. See?"

Alfonso is coming up the sidewalk, head down, his one hand in his pocket. Victor shakes his head, and his baby face pulls into a frown. I forgot he doesn't like Alfonso. I run to the front door and call to Alfonso. At first I think he's going to ignore me, but he hesitates then comes over.

"I'm so glad I saw you! I was going to stop by your house today, but I'm stuck at the store. My grandfather took ill."

"I'm sorry to hear that," Alfonso mumbles.

"I've got something to tell you. Can you come in? I have to stay close by in case my sister needs me."

Alfonso glances over my shoulder at Juanita. "I don't know, Miguel. I'm in a hurry. I'm leaving today."

"Leaving! Where?"

"I'm going to Houston to live with my aunt."

"But why? I thought you said you didn't want to take charity."

Alfonso glares at me. "What else am I supposed to do? The bank has taken the house. I need to get out."

"But that's what I want to talk to you about! I found you a job!"

At that moment, Juanita calls to me. "Miguel, fetch me a fresh egg for Mrs. Olson. This one is cracked."

I turn a pleading look on Alfonso. "Don't leave yet, okay? Just give me one minute and I'll explain."

Alfonso nods slowly and steps inside. He takes up his usual place by the vegetable bins, which reminds me that no one went to the market this morning. Abuelo wasn't here to do it. I set Victor down and tell him not to move. As I rush to the cooler, I kick myself. I should have had Rosa take me to the market as soon as Mamá called. I know how to pick the best vegetables. I know exactly what Abuelo would have looked for. I'll do it tomorrow morning, I promise myself as I run the egg back up to the counter. There will only be one day when J. Montoya's doesn't have the freshest produce in town. When I turn around, Alfonso is shifting impatiently from one foot to the other.

"We're really busy right now, and my papá's not here, but if you come back later today, you can talk to him about a job."

"What kind of job?"

"Keeping the books. It's math, Alfonso. If you can learn to hold your pencil in your left hand, you can do it. You'll see."

I watch Alfonso. His face shifts from skepticism to hope and then to something I don't expect, concern. "Where's your nephew?" he says.

I turn, and Victor is no longer by the cans. He's not by the counter, either. "Victor," I call. Juanita glances up. "Is Victor with you?" I ask hopefully. She shakes her head. I run past each of the aisles in our store, but there's no sign of him. I wonder if he followed someone into the cooler, but there's no one inside. I ask the butchers, but they haven't seen him. I'm getting worried now. So is Juanita. She's left her post at the counter.

"Where is he?" she demands. "Did you lose him?"

"No. He's here somewhere. I only took my eyes off him for a second."

"He didn't go out the front door, did he?"

My stomach churns. "No, I would have seen him. I was standing right by it."

"I'll check the storage room then. You check the back room."

Alfonso has joined me. He doesn't say anything, just searches the back room as I call for Victor. I try not to sound scared, but that's how I feel. Scared and angry. Why did I set him down? I should have kept him with me. I promised Ernesto I'd take care of his son. The back door to the store is open. We always keep it open in the summer to catch a breeze. But surely he couldn't have gotten outside so fast? Not on those little legs.

"Victor!" I call as I step outside. "Victoriano, answer me." There are plenty of sounds in the neighborhood this morning—cars starting, dogs barking, the milkman clinking bottles—but not the sound of a one-year-old's voice. Alfonso comes up behind me. "It'll be okay, Miguel. He can't have gone far."

My sister appears in the doorway. "Did you find

him yet?"

"No." I can't meet her eye.

"I'll find him. Miguel, go back up front and tell the customers to wait for me. Don't touch the register."

"No! I lost him. I'll find him."

Juanita wrings her hands. "Okay, keep looking. I'll lock the front door, then I'll come help you." She dashes back into the store.

"Maybe he went back to the house," Alfonso says.

Of course, that's what he must have done. I breathe a sigh of relief. He'd been wanting candy, so he probably went for Abuelita's candy dish in the parlor. We tear through the house, but Victor is not there. He's not anywhere.

I don't want to cry in front of Alfonso, but I can't help it. "Keep your head, brother," he says to me. "Think. Where else might he be?"

I shake my head. I can't think of a single place he might have gone. He's just a baby. I shade my eyes. Then I see something unusual—the Mueller's gate standing open, and I get a sinking feeling in my stomach. "Come on," I say, grabbing Alfonso by the arm. We push the gate open all the way, and I'm not too stunned to see half of our stash of scrap gone. Not the bigger pieces, like the lawn mower or the brass bed; the Wagner boys couldn't have made off with them on foot. But our smaller treasures are missing. In all the commotion last night with Abuelo, I forgot about the Wagner boys.

"Would Victor be here?" Alfonso says.

"Maybe. He's come with me lots of times when we drop things off. He likes to pick up the stuff and bang it on the pile. He likes the sound it makes."

Alfonso looks around. "Victor!"

"Victor!" I say.

And then we hear it, a muffled cry, an echo of a cry really. "Victor," I yell again, and I hear him say "Owie." My heart sinks.

"He's hurt! Where is he?!"

"There," Alfonso says. He points toward the open door to the coal chute that empties into the cellar below the house. I drop down on my knees and peer into the dark chute. "Victor?"

"Owie," he answers back, and I realize he's crying. Really crying.

"It's okay, Victor, we'll get you out."

Juanita is calling my name. "We're over here," I shout.

She comes around the corner of the house and

sees me on my knees. Her hands fly to her mouth. "*¡Ay Dios mío!* He's not down there, is he?"

I nod.

"We have to get down in the basement," she says. "Try the door, Miguel."

We try all the doors, but they're locked and the windows are boarded up. Alfonso is on his knees now, examining the chute.

"I'll have to go down," I say.

"You won't fit, Miguel," Juanita says, her voice nearly hysterical.

"I'm small. I can do it. I'll just slide down." I take a step toward the chute, but Alfonso blocks me with his arm.

"Stop," he says. "You're not thinking clearly."

"And you are?"

He smiles at me, a war-weary smile, and I remember then that he was a medic. As hard as it is for me to hear my little nephew crying, he must have heard a hundred wounded soldiers cry. I back away from his arm and take a deep breath. "Okay, Alfonso, what do we do?" I ask. Juanita gives me a dubious look. She glances at Alfonso and shakes her head as if to say *how can a one-armed man help us*, but she stays quiet.

"We need a rope," Alfonso says, turning to

Juanita.

"He's just a baby. He can't hold onto a rope," she snaps.

"I'm going to lower Miguel down the chute," Alfonso says calmly. "We need a rope to make sure he doesn't land on the baby and to pull him back up. Can you get me one? A long one? And a flashlight?"

"I don't think we own a flashlight," Juanita says.

"Yes we do. There's one at the store, in Papá's desk in the back."

Juanita nods. She jumps to her feet and races back to the house. There will be a rope in the shed. I know exactly which one. I used to try Roy Rogers rope tricks with it, pretending I was roping some villain. But this is no game. We've got to get Victor out of there.

"What do you want me to do?"

"He's hurt," Alfonso says. "When you get down there, you must tell me exactly what his wounds look like. Do you understand?"

"Yes."

"Okay, is there a song he likes to hear? A game he likes to play?"

"Um, I don't know. He likes 'Yankee Doodle.'"

"Okay, sing it. And keep singing it while I lower you down. It will help keep him calm."

I lower my mouth to the opening of the chute and sing, "Yankee Doodle went to town, a-riding on a pony . . ." I pause to listen. Victor's just whimpering now, but the sound breaks my heart. This is all my fault. I start to cry again. "Stay strong, brother," Alfonso says, and it's an order, not a request. I swallow my tears.

Juanita comes back with the rope and the flashlight, and Alfonso ties the rope securely under my arms. I swing my legs into the chute. "Now lie flat," he says. "Don't move. Just slide down the chute. Keep singing."

My voice sounds tinny in the coal chute as Alfonso and Juanita lower me down. I reach out with my feet, feeling for Victor, but he's backed up into the corner of the concrete bin. Smart baby!

"Hiya, Victor," I say, making my voice soft and soothing. "Look what I've got." I click on the flashlight and see my nephew sucking his fingers, big tears making tracks in the coal dust on his cheeks. He's sitting up, but his leg beneath his knee is twisted at an odd angle.

"How does he look?" Alfonso calls down.

"His leg looks funny. And he's not moving it."

"What else?"

"He's got some scrapes on his hands and legs and a little bump on his head, but he looks okay. He wants me to pick him up."

"No, don't. We've got to keep his leg still. It could be broken. I'm going to break some wood off the fence. Do you know how to make a splint?"

"Yeah, we learned in Boy Scouts."

"Good. Put the splint on his leg and we'll pull him up."

"Okay," I say. "But he's not gonna like it."

Alfonso gives a half-laugh. I hear him tell Juanita to talk to Victor, to promise him candy, to keep talking until he comes up. Alfonso slides the wood down the chute. He's cut some lengths off the end of the rope and he slides those down too. I take a deep breath and lay Victor down. I give him the flashlight to play with. He's still crying, but not as hard. I work the ropes around his leg as gently as I can, trying hard to remember what Gary's father, our Boy Scout leader, had shown us. "Good boy, Victor," I say. He really is tough, this kid. When the splint is on, I tie the rope under his arms and tell him he has to be very still. I reach for the flashlight, but he won't give it up. He's cradling it to his chest like it's his stuffed bunny, so I let him have it. I lift him gently into the chute and

Juanita and Alfonso start to pull him carefully up.

When he reaches the top, Juanita lifts him gently out of the chute. Through the opening, I see Alfonso carefully remove the rope. He looks at Victor's leg. "Yep, it's broken. Take him to the house and call the doctor. Try not to move his leg."

"What about Miguel?"

"I'll get him out."

"By yourself?"

Alfonso follows her gaze to his missing limb. A slow smile spreads across his face. "By myself," he assures her.

"Thank you," Juanita says, and through the opening in the chute, I see her give Alfonso a quick kiss on the cheek. He watches her leave, then throws the rope back down. I tie it around my chest under my arms.

"Okay, see if you can push yourself up the chute with your feet a little as I pull," Alfonso says. "I'm going to wrap this rope around a tree for some leverage, so when you feel me tug, start pushing."

I inch my way up the coal chute. If I'd been much bigger, I never would have made it through this tight squeeze. When I reach the top, I grab onto the outer edge of the chute and pull myself out. Alfonso joins me.

"Is he gonna be okay?" I ask.

"He'll be fine. Don't worry."

"What am I gonna tell Rosa? This is all my fault."

"It was an accident, Miguel. They'll understand that."

"No. They left me in charge, and I blew it."

"You didn't blow it. You got him out, didn't you?"

"With your help."

"It was nothing."

"But it *was* something. If you hadn't been here, I would have just jumped into that chute and then what? We'd have both been stuck. I don't think things through all the way. That's why they won't let me run the register. But you knew what to do, Alfonso. There *are* things you can do. Even with only one arm. You can work for my father and maybe for some other folks too. You can't just go and live with your aunt. You can't give up. My brother would never give up, even if he broke every bone in his body jumping from that airplane."

The tears are falling freely now, and I don't care if he sees them. They're tears of relief for my nephew, worry for my grandfather and my brother, and shame for my mistake. I figure I earned them. Alfonso drapes his arm across my shoulders.

"Okay, kid. I'll talk to your father. But I gotta find me a place to stay first. They came for my house this morning."

"Couldn't you talk to the bank? If they know you've got a job, maybe they'll give you more time."

"No, I'm afraid my time is up, Miguel. *Está bien.* A house is a lot of work to keep up. Think I'll rent me a room till I get back on my feet. I'll need your help, though, moving some of my things."

"You got it," I say, wiping my tears with the back of my sleeve.

"Let's go check on your nephew," Alfonso says, closing the lid to the coal chute this time. "That your scrap heap?"

"It was. Looks like the Wagner boys got to it last night. Guess there's no hope for the contest now."

"Sorry to hear it. Hey, Miguel, where would I be doing the books?"

"In the back room, why?"

"Just wondering. Seems like Juanita's always up front though, right? At the register?"

"Ah, do you have to be stuck on *her*?" I say. "I'm glad school is starting. If I had to watch you makin' eyes at my sister all day, I'd chuck up for sure."

Alfonso just laughs.

12

V for Victory

Papá backs the delivery truck into the alley and right up near the Mueller's back fence. He drops the tailgate, and I help him lift the brass headboard into the bed of the truck. Then I rush back for the lawn mower. "Looks like that thing has seen better days," Papá says as I roll it squeaking and squealing up to the truck. "What else you got?"

"Not much," I say. "Just a few things Alfonso cleared out of his house. The Wagner boys got the rest."

"Now, Miguel, you don't know for sure it was them."

"We'd know if you would have gone with me to their house to check."

"The Wagners are regular customers. We can't go accusing their boys with no proof."

I don't need proof to know it was them, but

there's no use arguing. Papá's mind is made up. And I've been on my best behavior since the accident with Victor. Trying to make up for what I did, I guess, though no one's held it against me. To my astonishment, Juanita told them it was as much her fault as mine, and since Victor wound up with only a small fracture, no one stayed too upset for long, especially when later that day a letter arrived special delivery from a member of Ernesto's bomber squadron. He said he'd seen Ernesto's plane go down and the crew bail out. He wanted us to know how much my brother was loved and respected by his comrades and how much they were pulling for him. He couldn't give any more details, but just hearing that Ernesto had made it out of the plane gave us hope. We'll hear from the Red Cross or the army telling us where he is, I just know it. Rosa's written him at least a dozen letters already and is just waiting to hear where to send them. I've written one or two myself.

Papá runs back to the house to get his wallet. Lucky comes sauntering up.

"Hiya, Luck."

"Need help?" he asks.

"Already done. Not much to load." I stare at the

ground. "I forgot to tell you, Lucky. The Wagner boys stole our stash."

Lucky shakes his head. "Real sorry to hear that. Guess you won't be getting that bike now."

The bike. I'd forgotten all about it. Seems so unimportant now.

"And you won't be getting your glasses."

"Oh I got that all worked out."

"How?"

"Mr. Garza's cough has gotten worse. He's taken to his bed. Doc say he'll likely finish out his days there."

I shake my head. "Can't picture Mr. Garza gone. He's been sitting in that lawn chair as long as I can remember."

"And he aims to be back there no matter what the doc say. He might jest do it too. That man is stubborn as a mule. But for now, he givin' me five cents a day to watch his property."

I laugh. "He sure is crazy 'bout his yard."

"Mama say Mr. Garza was born hardscrabble poor in Mexico. He never dreamed he'd own a house as fine as that one. Never has gotten over bein' proud of it."

"How you gonna watch it when school starts?"

"Guess I go by there before school and when I come home for lunch. And I'll sit there of an evenin' and keep the kids off his yard."

I frown. "What about the Wagner boys? You can't stand up to them."

"Well, when there comes a need, I can run pretty fast."

Lucky helps me close the tailgate to the truck, and we stand on the tires to look in. "We could have won if I could have gotten that fence," I say.

"Or Mr. Garza's jalopy."

"Guess your luck wasn't with us this time," I say.

"Oh I don't know," Lucky says, hopping down. "Found this penny on the sidewalk on the way over. Heads up."

"See you at the movies, Luck," I say.

"Yeah, see ya."

I don't think to offer Lucky a ride. He'll take the bus to the theater with his friends, sitting in the back with the other Negros, and then he'll watch the movies from the colored section in the fifth-floor balcony while Gary and I sit below.

When we pull into Gary's drive, Papá gets out to return Mrs. Bauer's casserole dish for Mamá. Gary grabs my arm. "Come up and see the model."

"Now? But we gotta hurry."

"There's time. My mother will talk your father's ear off for at least five minutes."

We bound upstairs to Gary's room. He flings the door open and lifts the model carefully off his desk, grinning from ear to ear. I take my cue from Gary and whistle appreciatively. "Wow, that's a humdinger, Gary." He hands it to me, and I turn it from side to side, admiring the shiny stickers on the wings, twisting the propeller, peering into the tiny plastic windows, and imagining I can see the pilot inside. "Where you gonna put this one?"

"Don't know. I'm kinda running out of room. Thought maybe you could hang it up in your room for me. Maybe over Victor's crib. But you gotta hang it high. Wouldn't want him tearing it down."

"I can't take your plane, Gary," I say.

"Oh I'm not givin' it to you. Just asking you to store it for me for a while. Just till I figure out a place for it."

I grin. "Okay. I'll pick it up after the movies. You can come for supper and help me hang it. Victor will love it."

I set the model plane down gently on his desk. "Got something else for you too," he says. "Hold out your hand."

I do as he tells me, and he lays the piece of wing from the plane wreck on my palm. "Put it on the scrap pile. Won't make up for what the Wagner brothers stole, but it'll help." Gary's face is red, and I know he feels responsible for our lost loot. This is his way of making up for it. "I've been thinking a lot about the co-pilot who died in the crash, the one from our neighborhood. There's a gold star in his family's window now. You were right. I shouldn't keep it."

I smile at my friend and close my hand around the piece of wing. "Thanks, Gary."

My father calls to us and we leave the room, pulling the chain on the overhead light as we go.

At the theater, the kids have already started lining up. Being first in line is always a big deal. Some of the kids are holding sacks of scrap, others have brought wagons along. The manager is telling them to wait till the doors open and they can pile their stuff in the lobby. Papá leans out the window of the truck and says, "What about us?" He indicates the bed of the truck with his thumb. The manager looks flustered as the Wagner truck pulls up behind ours. Papá and Mr. Wagner climb out as the manager scratches his head.

"Well now, you can't bring all that stuff inside. You'll have to drive it down to Municipal Auditorium and dump it there. Let me see first who's got the most."

Gary and I scramble out of the truck and stand on the tires as the manager inspects our load. From this height, we can see into the bed of Mr. Wagner's truck, and there's the furnace all right, cut down to pieces and lying amidst the other scrap. While the theater manager is dealing with another truck that has pulled up front, my father waves me over to the Wagner truck.

"Fine load you boys got here," Papá says, leaning his arms on the slats of the truck. "I don't suppose anyone will beat this."

The Wagner boys don't answer.

"Awfully good of your uncle to donate that furnace. Looks like a few other people pitched in too," he says, and reaching into the bed of the truck, he pulls up a shiny, almost new bedpan that could only have come from the Sisters of the Holy Ghost. So my father *had* been paying attention all this time. "I thought it was awfully clever of you boys to go in on this with Miguel and Gary. Nice of you to keep so much of it at your house too. We don't have much room at ours these days. Course, it means you'll have to split the twenty dollars four ways, but it's worth it in the end if you win, right? And it's for the war effort."

Tug puffs out his chest like he's gonna say something. Though he's only fourteen years old, he's already taller than my father. But just then, Mr. Wagner strides over.

"Afternoon, Herb," my father says. "Just congratulating your boys. Real smart for them to go in with my son and his friend to get as much as they could. Many hands make light work, isn't that how the Anglo saying goes?"

Mr. Wagner glances at his sons, but they both look away. As understanding spreads across his face, he turns to my father and nods. "You tell Miguel to come by this evening, and I'll make sure he gets his share."

"I'll do that. Guess we better take our loads to the auditorium."

Tug and his brother sneer at me as we pass.

"You boys better steer clear of those two for a while," Papá says, but his warning is unnecessary. We've been steering clear of the Wagner boys for years. As I run around to hop into the cab of the truck, Papá says, "Why don't you boys stay here. Get

142

in line for the movies. I can manage on my own."

"You sure, Papá?"

"I'm sure."

"Thanks, Papá!" I say, and we scramble into the drugstore to load up on popcorn and candy for a long afternoon.

After the matinee, Rosa picks us up in the car. She's been running errands downtown. As she pulls up to the curb, Victor's head pops up in the window. He pulls himself up and bounces up and down in his excitement to see us, the cast on his leg doing little to slow him down. Rosa pulls him onto her lap as Gary and I push the front seat forward and climb in back. There will be no Cokes today. We're going home. Abuelo is coming home tonight, and we're all going to eat supper together. Not even Juanita is going out.

As the car rolls through town, Victor stands on the seat looking out the window. Rosa tells me to keep a hold of his shirt so he won't fall out. Gary and I are filling her in on the movie when the crossing arms come down at the railroad tracks, and a troop train rolls slowly in front of the car. I heave myself over the seat and sit on the ledge of the car window, pulling Victor up beside me.

"Choo, choo," he says.

"That's right, Victor. Choo Choo."

"Daddy," he says, and I see him pointing to the soldiers in their uniforms leaning out the train windows and waving back.

I push his finger down gently and lock eyes with Rosa. "No, Victor, not Daddy," I say, and I remember what Abuelo said about all the soldiers he'd seen in his lifetime, all the trains full of men going off to war. All the women and children they left behind. I think about Alfonso and the medals he showed me now packed away in a box, and I wonder how old Victor will be when the war ends. I remember Rosa telling us his name when he was born. "Victoriano," she had said. "He's my little good luck charm. He'll bring us victory so his daddy can come home." I look at Victor and hope that's still true, that one day we'll all be gathered around the table again—Papá and Mamá, Abuelo and Abuelita, Tía Silvia and Carlos, Juanita, Victor, Rosa and me—to welcome Ernesto home. I take Victor's pudgy fingers and form them into the V for Victory sign. I hold his hand up high so the soldiers can see it. One soldier sends us a V back and it's good to see, but Victor just sticks his fingers in his mouth. I shake my head at him.

"Guess what I saved for you, Victor?" I say, and I pull a half-eaten roll of NECCO Wafers from my pocket. All of a sudden, I wrinkle my nose and lower him gently back to the seat.

"Oh brother," Gary says as the smell reaches the back seat.

"Now you boys be nice," Rosa scolds. "Someone changed your dirty diapers once, you know."

As the train rolls by and the crossing arms go up, we sit in the back seat holding our noses and laughing as Victor gobbles up the candy.

Meet the Real Miguel Montoya

Roman Talamantez

As with all of my books, *V for Victory* was inspired by
the memories of a real person, in this case my uncle
Roman Talamantez. Like Miguel in the story, Roman
spent his early childhood in San Antonio, Texas. And
like Miguel, he had a large extended family. He used
to enjoy helping at his uncle's grocery store, doing
all of the things Miguel does in this book: stocking
shelves, dusting cans, sweeping floors, etc. And he,
too, wasn't allowed to run the cash register and *hated*
his short haircut.

Unlike Miguel, Roman was the oldest child in his
family, but he remembers worrying about his uncle,
who was serving in the navy, and about the husbands
and boyfriends of his aunts, one of whom—like
Ernesto—was shot down over Germany. Roman
never had a bothersome little nephew to baby-sit, but
he did have twin baby sisters, my mom and my aunt.

And Uncle Roman loved to go to Saturday
matinees with his friends and he really did see Roy

Rogers at the theater. Like many boys his age, he could recognize all the military planes by sight. As a child, he enjoyed taking things apart to see how they worked and often fiddled with his kite to see if he could make it fly better. That curious kid grew up to work with radar equipment in the army and later earned a college degree in electrical engineering.

Though his career took him to different parts of the country, and even onto a ship that sailed the Pacific and Atlantic oceans, he now lives back in Texas, in the city of Houston. He's seventy-four years old and has a son and two granddaughters.

If you want to know what my uncle looked like when he was young, check out the illustration on the front cover. That's him!

And the baby is actually drawn to look exactly like my son, Brian, when he was that age. That's only fair since my daughter Lydia is on the cover of my book *Doing My Part*.

If You'd Been Friends with Miguel Montoya

If you'd been friends with Miguel Montoya, you might have:

Gone to SATURDAY MATINEES. In the time before televisions in every home and long before computers or video games, children looked forward to Saturday movie matinees. They'd come from all over town to stand in line for tickets, stopping first at a corner drugstore to buy candy, popcorn, sodas, and sometimes hot dogs. Even the biggest movie palaces overflowed with kids. Sometimes you'd have to share your seat with a sibling or friend. The projectionist would first run the newsreel, then a cartoon, then a serial. Serials were like long movies shown in short episodes each week. They were often Westerns or featured science fiction characters (like Flash Gordon) or cartoon characters (like Batman), and they always ended in a "cliffhanger" that made you want to come back next week to see what happened. After the serial came the double feature—two movies back to back. Children Miguel's age loved the Western movies. And big stars, like Roy Rogers, Tex Ritter, and Gene Autry would sometimes visit theaters to meet their young fans. Kids loved the matinees so much that some would arrive around eleven o'clock for the first round of films and then sit through the whole thing again!

Participated in SCRAP DRIVES. Due to the war and rationing, there were shortages of many things, and the government called on citizens to collect and recycle needed materials. Rubber drives, scrap metal drives, silk drives, and paper drives were common during the war, and though everyone was encouraged to participate, it was children who really stepped forward to help! They lined up to deposit cooking fats their mothers had saved, which were turned into glycerin to make explosives. And like Miguel, children also scoured their neighborhoods looking for old scrap metal, which was melted down to make planes, ships, and weapons. The Boy Scouts alone helped collect more than 54,000 tons of old bike and car tires for rubber drives. And kids even pestered their mothers to donate their silk and nylon stockings to be used to make parachutes and tow ropes for gliders.

Written lots of LETTERS. In the 1940s, much of the technology we use today hadn't been invented yet. If you wanted to communicate with someone far away, the best way to do so was in a letter. Soldiers eagerly awaited mail call because those letters made them feel less lonely. People on the home front knew that. Some of them, like Miguel's sister, Juanita, wrote letters to several soldiers to keep their spirits up. In this story, Miguel uses a special type of stationery called V-mail (or Victory Mail) to write to his brother, Ernesto. V-mail was designed to save space so more letters would fit on cargo ships and arrive more quickly. Hundreds of millions of both regular letters and V-mail were sent to soldiers during World War II, and just as many were written by the soldiers and sent back home. People rushed to their mailboxes every day looking for letters from the men and women who'd gone off to war.

Displayed a BLUE STAR in your window. The Blue Star Service Banner (like the one shown on the cover of this book) was designed during World War I but used more commonly in World War II. Anyone who had a member of their immediate family—like a father, brother, husband, or son—serving in the war could hang a Blue Star Banner in their window. The blue star always appeared on a field of white surrounded by a red border. Some had fringe or other minor decorations. If you had more than one member of your family serving, you could sew more than one star on your banner. And if your loved one was killed, you changed the blue star to a gold one. Many people recall feeling sad when they passed homes displaying gold stars in the windows. Though in some ways World War II was an exciting time to be a kid, those stars reminded children that war brings many losses.

Glossary

Abuela – grandmother

Abuelo – grandfather

Anglo – another word for white people

Ay – expression that refers to sorrow, pity or concern

Ay Dios mío – oh my Lord

Buenas tardes – good afternoon

Buenos días – good morning

Cabrito – the meat of a young goat

Café con leche – coffee with milk

Comino – cumin seed spice

Empanadas – a type of pastry

Empanadas de calabaza – a pumpkin pastry

Empanadas de camote – a sweet potato pastry

Es lo primero – "the thing that comes first"

Está bien – it's all right

Fiesta – party

Jap – a common but unkind term during the war for people of Japanese ancestry

Kraut – a common but unkind term during the war for people of German ancestry

La Revolución – the Mexican Revolution

Mamá – mother

Mercado – market

Mijo – my son

Pan dulce – sweet bread

Panadería – bakery

Papá – father

Perdón, señorita – pardon me, miss

Picadillo – a Mexican dish made mostly with ground beef and sometimes vegetables

Piñatas – a figure made from a clay pot (and later from papier-mâché or cardboard) filled with candy and toys that children break open with a stick

Pozole – a Mexican dish made with hominy, pork, and spices

¿Que hay de cenar, Abuelita? – what's for dinner, Grandma?

Señor – mister

Señorita – miss

Sí – yes

Siesta – a nap

Tamales – a Mexican dish made with meat, cheese, or chilies wrapped in corn dough

Tienda – store

Tortilla – a round flatbread made from corn or wheat

Un momento – just a minute

Un nombre fuerte – a strong name

Yo te lo compro – I'll buy it for you

About the Author

Teresa R. Funke writes for children and adults. Most of her books and short stories are based on real people and actual events, and many are set in World War II. She says, "I chose *V for Victory* for my third book in the Home-Front Heroes series because I wanted my readers to see that we all have amazing stories within our own families. All we have to do is ask! I was excited to share a bit of history in this book from my mom's Mexican-American family. The Home-Front Heroes series was created in part to celebrate the World War II contributions of people of various races, creeds, and religions. We have all helped build this wonderful melting pot we call America. Kids too!"

Teresa also enjoys speaking at schools and conferences and working with writers as a writers' coach, but what she likes best is spending time with her husband and three children at their home in Colorado. She'd love it if you visited her website at **www.teresafunke.com** to submit your own family's stories from World War II or other time periods, or to invite Teresa to speak at your school or visit your class via webcast!!

Coming Soon From Teresa R. Funke

The Newest Home-Front Hero

As the only Jewish girl in her New York neighborhood, thirteen-year-old Miriam Liebler has a lot on her mind. World War II is raging, and her brother is fighting overseas. At home, blackouts and air-raid drills have become part of her daily life. Worse yet, her family hasn't heard from their Jewish relatives in Europe since before the war started, and Miriam suspects the worst. None of her friends truly understand her worries, until she meets Christopher Gifford, an English boy sent by his parents to America to escape the deadly bombings taking place in London. Miriam and Christopher exchange candy, comic books, and secret fears through the iron bars of the orphanage fence, but will their friendship survive when bad news finally arrives?

CPSIA information can be obtained at www.ICGtesting.com
Printed in the USA
LVOW011615090112

263056LV00011B/51/P